The Darkened Room

The Darkened Room

Also by Antonia Hildebrand and published by Ginninderra Press
The Blind Colossus
To Breathe
War Stories
A Simple Twist of Fate

Antonia Hildebrand

The Darkened Room

The Darkened Room
ISBN 978 1 76109 268 8
Copyright © text Antonia Hildebrand 2022
Cover: Maryann Hine using resources from Freepik.com

First published 2022 by
GINNINDERRA PRESS
PO Box 3461 Port Adelaide 5015
www.ginninderrapress.com.au

Everything is Prologue: October 1992

'I'll kill him, I will! I will!' she said, and began crying. The friend she said this to testified against her in court.

Leonora Davison was a tall, heavy-set blonde who had once been beautiful and the man she was threatening to kill was her ex-husband, Sam Davison. A man who had discarded her for another woman. A woman he subsequently married. A younger woman, of course, who looked the way Leonora had when she was a young newly-wed. The new woman's name was Susan and she had the same thick, wavy blonde hair and the same beautiful blue eyes as Leonora – but she had a lithe, lean frame and firm, tanned skin. She was twenty-five; Leonora was forty-one. When Leonora loved, it was for keeps. As Sam Davison would eventually learn. Davison was a wealthy, handsome man, a doctor. Things had always come easily to him and when he had no further use for them, he simply let them go. Leonora could not do that. That was her tragedy and she would make it his.

Killing Sam

Early in the morning of 3 November 1992, a white Chevrolet Suburban four-wheel drive turned on to an empty street and stopped at the two-storey brick house near the end of Banksia Avenue. Sam was a dashing dresser who wore only custom-tailored suits and had a top hat and cape for more formal occasions but Leonora turned up to kill Sam and his new wife, Susan, wearing casual clothes and loafers. However, she also wore a diamond necklace and earrings. She was not well and she had a gun.

Upstairs, Sam and Susan were asleep. Sam wore only boxer shorts. Susan was nude. Leonora knew the children were spending the night at Sam's mother's place and she was taking them to school the next day. Shane, her son, had told her during a phone call.

To get to the bedroom, Leonora had to get through a locked door. Susan knew Sam had started a war with Leonora and insisted they sleep, as if in a fortress, with the bedroom door locked – even though Sam mocked her for it. She had seen Leonora with a gun in her hand (aimed at her) and seen how well she handled it and how powerful she looked with a gun in her hand. But, unfortunately, Leonora knew the house. The housekeeper had let her in when her employers and the children weren't home because she was too afraid of Leonora to refuse and then was too afraid to tell her employers what she had done. Leonora had strolled through every room, upstairs and down. She knew that if she went through a small study next to the bathroom, she could enter the bedroom through another door.

To her surprise, although she believed she had made virtually no noise, the minute she entered the room, Sam woke like a sleeping cat and Susan woke too and started screaming. Both of them could see the gun in her hand. Sam yelled, 'Call the police!' But nothing was going to save either of them. They just didn't know it yet.

Leonora started firing and as she did she made a tremendous exhalation. A noise like 'AAAAAAAH'. As if all the pain, the hate, the rejection was flying out of her. As if toxins were leaving her body. She fired five times, though she only remembered firing once and only remembered that a long time later. Strange, she thought, that she hit them with every shot. It was so dark in the room she could only make out dim shapes. Sam had tried to grab the phone but Leonora wrenched it away from him, pulled it out of the wall and threw it on the floor. Susan was hit in the head and her beautiful body lay tangled in bloody sheets. She died instantly. Sam was hit in the back, arm and leg, and a bullet also entered his lungs. He died thirty minutes after he was shot. He was never able to call the police.

Later, she tried to explain over and over that, yes, she was crazy when she shot them but that Sam had deliberately made her that way and then used it to take everything away from her. Her house, her self-esteem, her dignity and finally her children. He just never understood that a crazy woman was a danger. He despised her so utterly he never thought she was actually capable of killing him. It was on these grounds that her lawyer considered it to be manslaughter, not murder. Leonora was never prepared for the cold flipside of love. Her entire life had been Sam and her children. His needs trumped hers and she had never been prepared as a girl for anything other than being a wife and mother. Nor did she actually want to be anything else. Losing Sam meant losing her life's work, her purpose in life, her sense of herself. The way he treated her, when he decided to throw her away, destroyed her. In her mind, she had no choice but to destroy him so that she could survive. Like a child striking out, she removed him from the woman who had taken him from her and also killed her rival.

It wasn't rational. Nothing about it was rational. Why couldn't anyone understand that? Her bond to him was not only emotional, it was sexual. And once sex rears its lovely head, all bets are off. Nothing she did was logical but sex is not logical. They didn't seem to understand that either.

A Shopping Spree

She had Sam's wallet with all his credit cards, his licence and a photo (a selfie) taken on the beach of him holding Susan in his arms, both of them smiling and glowing with the Look of Love. She had taken the wallet from a dresser in the bedroom after firing the shots.

Later, the police asked her sneeringly how she could see it if the room was so dark. It held his gold credit card. She decided to go shopping, as she always did when she was stressed. She was angrier than she had ever been in her life. 'What has he made me do? Why can't I remember?' she said over and over again as she drove down town and parked in a multi-storey car park.

The first thing she needed was chocolate. So she headed to a coffee shop that sold handmade chocolates, ordered a coffee and an expensive box of chocolates. But they were for later. Now, she wanted a slice of double chocolate and caramel cheesecake. She wanted sex too, naturally, because for her sex and chocolate went together. Later, she would see about that, too. Why should she be monogamous when it seemed everyone else was not? She sipped the coffee and spooned the cheesecake into her mouth, savouring every bite. She knew she was out of control but she found she kind of liked it. Leaving the coffee shop, she turned her steps to a shopping mall that she knew had a lot of very expensive boutiques.

First Sweet Temptation, which sold lingerie. The salesgirls looked at her generous curves and hid their smiles reasonably well. She bought three very expensive teddies of lace and ribbons – black, white and red. If Sam was dead, she was going to jail but not without one last glorious splurge. Happiness and consumption were now one and the same in her mind. He had cheated her out of money but now she had his credit card and he had no say.

As Leonora wandered down the mall, hitting one shop after another – clothes, handbags, jewellery, perfume: there was nothing she didn't want – Sam's mother, Glenys, arrived at his house for a prearranged outing with Susan. The front door was hanging open. Glenys was a widow. She lived alone and enjoyed outings.

'That's strange,' she thought, still with a cheerful smile on her face. Since he got rid of crazy Leonora, everything was going swimmingly. She had never liked her.

'Hello? Anyone here?' she called, checking her watch. Yes, it was nine thirty a.m., the time they had arranged.

The silence suddenly seemed very ominous. She could hear a clock ticking, she could hear the birds chirping and fussing outside the window. Normally, Sam would be on his way to work and Susan was an early riser, she would have been up for hours, but she wasn't in the kitchen or the lounge and both their cars were in the garage when she went and checked. How odd. Calling their names, she slowly walked up the carpeted stairs. There was a strange, sickly smell in the air. She didn't know that it was blood until she got to the top of the stairs and looked into the bedroom. Everything swam, then, and she thought she would collapse. Flies were crawling on their bloodied faces. Their eyes were open and flies were all around them, moving like eyelashes. She turned, screaming, and ran down the stairs.

While Sam's mother called the police, Leonora was in Sophisticated Lady having her nails done. She had made three trips to the car so far to put all her purchases in the back. Then she made her way to Café Noir, a favourite place for lunch in the days when Sam still loved her, or pretended he did. As she sat waiting for her meal to arrive, a man at the bar began giving her the eye. She wasn't used to this any more and put her head down at first but then she remembered that having sex was part of her splurge. She lifted her head and smiled at him. Catching sight of herself in the mirror behind the bar, she could see that she looked quite pretty. The chocolate, the lingerie, the endless spending had excited her.

He came over to sit at her table. 'Mind if I join you?' he asked, with a knowing grin.

'Of course not,' she said. Was it so obvious that she was available? But then she thought, 'What the hell. Soon I'll be in jail and it might be for a very long time. I might as well enjoy myself and if he's a serial killer, it will save the state a fortune.' She stifled a laugh.

He was looking at her, studying her face and body but she didn't care about that either.

She had a bottle of Moët sitting in an ice bucket by her chair. 'Like a drink?' she asked him and he nodded, still smiling.

He was fair-haired, in his fifties, she thought, with very blue eyes and lovely hands with long fingers. Tall and slim. He had generous pink lips and his mouth curved up at either end. A lucky mouth, she thought. No wedding band but she guessed he was someone's husband. So what? Someone had had her husband, it was only fair. The black teddy, she thought, would be the one he would like to see her in.

Soon they were in a hotel room and she was wearing the black teddy and eating chocolates – until he took the chocolate box out of her hands, took the teddy off her and climbed on top of her. He sucked her breasts, first one then the other, and put his finger up inside her, moving it backwards and forwards in a slow, practised way. She ran her hands all over him and kissed his neck and his chest. He liked that very much and pinned her to the pillow in a passionate kiss, all his weight on her as he rubbed his penis on her thighs. He was an experienced and vigorous lover and she came three times. Then he got out of bed naked and walked to the bathroom to take a shower. He was muscled and tanned – obviously fond of the gym and the beach. Then he put his clothes on and left – after planting a lingering kiss on her lips. He took her number but she was sure he would never call. A good thing too, since she was going to be arrested for murder. He told her his name was Ian, but it probably wasn't. She reached for the chocolate box. Saw by the clock on the wall that it was now two p.m.

The police were swarming all over Sam's house, and Sam's mother had gone to pick the children up from school so that they wouldn't come home to this nightmare.

'Leonora did this,' Sam's mother told the police with tears in her eyes. 'His ex-wife.'

Then she left to pick up the children and take them to her place. She also gave the police Leonora's address but Leonora was sleeping by that time, in a plush hotel room with an empty chocolate box on the floor, where she had tossed it. The man who might or might not be called Ian had paid with his credit card for the room. She told him her name was Tania Smith. It didn't help. Her face was all over the TV news and someone in the hotel saw her getting out of the elevator. She saw the news herself and fled the hotel. She was a wanted woman after being unwanted for so long. Ironic.

On the Run

'I had no clue where to go or what to do,' she told police after her arrest.

They weren't really interested in that but they feigned interest hoping she would confess.

She didn't know if her shots, fired in a darkened room, had hit anyone. She had not seen Susan lying nude and bloodied, tangled in the sheets that had trapped her as she tried to run.

'You mean you didn't see his wife lying there wrapped in the sheets?' a police officer asked her.

'No. I didn't,' she said, coldly. Even now the word 'wife' rankled. She was his wife, always would be.

'Why did you do it?' another one said, trying his luck. 'Where's the gun?'

'I'm not saying anything more without my lawyer. Not a word,' she told them.

They knew she meant it and let her call her lawyer while they watched her in stony silence. They thought she was a monster. She wasn't even shaking. Wasn't even crying. They didn't know she had already done all that and was now icy calm. One thing was certain, she told herself: she was not spending the rest of her life in prison. They would never find the gun.

After she fled the hotel, she spent that first night sleeping in her car. The next morning, she drove to a café for an omelette and a badly needed coffee. No one recognised her. She looked terrible: nothing like the glamorous photo they were using on the front page of the papers. Then she aimlessly wandered the streets like a lost soul, stopping her wandering only to have lunch in another café. Eventually, she came to a park and a bridal couple came out of it, all dressed in their wedding regalia, and got into a white limo also decorated in wedding finery. They were young and beautiful and so much in love they couldn't keep their hands off each other. She watched them kissing in the back seat of the limo. Then the wedding guests spilled out on to the footpath too and also watched them. Some of them threw confetti while other guests told them not to do it – no confetti allowed on the footpath.

As the limo drove away, Leonora realised she was crying. Only now, in that moment, did the full force of what she had lost hit her. She had had it all but somehow the fates had decreed that it would all be taken away from her. She looked after the limo gliding down the street like a magic machine and she wished them luck. She knew they would need it.

The wedding guests now started fanning out in search of their own cars to go to the reception. With tears in her eyes, she tried to phone Ellen Brown but it rang out so she trudged wearily on. She had no idea where she thought she was going but deep down inside she knew all of this could only end one way: with her in jail, at least in the short term.

She had at first thought Sam was still alive and most likely calling the police and had been sick with terror.All she could really remember was getting into the house and walking up the stairs. Suddenly, she understood that the idea that Sam could die was actually inconceivable to her. God couldn't die. She wasn't going home because she knew the police would go there looking for her and she wanted freedom for as long as she could get it. In the incredibly long and nasty custody battle, Sam had won, as he had won every other round. Sam had gained full custody of the boys, Shane aged eleven and Thomas aged ten, and the girls had been living at Sam's place for some time now. If she hadn't killed him, she would have had to hand them all over to Sam and hope that he would let her see them after months of separation. Hard to believe now that ten years ago she and Sam had been regularly having sex – which had led to Thomas's conception. It seemed like a lost paradise. So far removed from the hell she had been plunged into and was still in.

Finally, she managed to call Ellen Brown from a phone booth near Martin Place. Crying, almost hysterical, she tried to make Ellen understand the ghastly situation she was in, the unthinkable things she might have done.

'What do you mean, you don't know if you killed Sam? What are you talking about?' Ellen said, calmly and reasonably.

For some reason, this made Leonora break down completely. She sobbed and howled and, while she was doing that, all she could think about was the last time she and Sam had shared a bed and made love. She remembered him kissing her as she was holding his erect penis in her hand. The way he kissed her and the way he felt inside her remained vivid. Orgasm made her feel as if she couldn't breathe. So hard to believe that meeting Susan had made him forget all that and start to hate her. But it had. Only hate could have made him act as he had.

'Where are you?' Ellen asked.

'In hell,' she wailed and hung up.

In the course of the conversation, she told Ellen that she thought she had fired a gun. She couldn't quite remember. Ellen testified to that effect in court. Ellen had always been plain. She had no idea what it was like to be beautiful and have the world at your feet on account of it. And she didn't have to experience losing that beauty and then having everything that made your life worth living taken away from you. Ellen did not have to endure her husband's new wife sending her ads for wrinkle creams or brochures from weight loss clinics. Both Sam and Susan had waged war on Leonora. Ellen had been spared this particular mockery: she had been the plain friend of the beautiful girl since their high school days so she had been mocked – just not in the way Leonora had. Most beautiful girls had a friend like this except when they had a friend who was as beautiful as they were – then they could cause a riot just walking into a bar or a club. Leonora and a girl called Maya Devereux sometimes did that just for the attention. As dark as Leonora was fair, Maya was exquisite and enjoyed being the centre of a fuss. They did it for laughs.

In court, Ellen described Leonora as 'distraught' and 'incoherent'. She told the court that Leonora had also said, 'Anyway, you know how it was. It was them or me.'

Then, in a moment of devastating clarity, she told Ellen Brown, 'Now I think I can remember. I shot them both. He was gurgling. But I don't remember if he was dead.'

But Brown only testified in court that Leonora told her she wanted to kill herself.

Eventually, Ellen and Leonora met up and Leonora went to the West Ryde police station and turned herself in, with Ellen at her side. She took off the diamond earrings and her diamond-encrusted watch and the diamond necklace. She gave them to Ellen. Her marriage to Sam had lasted fifteen years but no one could have predicted that the golden couple would end up in a bloody mess. Or that one of them would end up dead.

'Take all those things to Lifeline. I don't want them,' she told Ellen as they got out of the car at the police station, indicating all the numerous shopping bags in the back seat. All the luxury items she had bought on her crazed shopping spree.

'And get rid of this,' Leonora said, slipping the credit card into her hand. 'Cut it up and throw it away.' She had already thrown Sam's wallet in an industrial bin at the back of a shop.

Ellen did as she was told.

Only a psychopath could go on a shopping spree after shooting two people. That was what a jury would think. But shopping had always been Leonora's consolation. It consoled her when Sam didn't want her and it consoled her after she shot him. And sex with a stranger in a hotel room? What a dent that would make in the good girl image she wanted to project. And the image of her sitting in Café Noir sipping

Moët after the murders and on the prowl for a man would also be disastrous. It all proved that she was not in her right mind, not herself when she fired that gun, but no jury, she was sure, would see it that way. The police soon established that numerous purchases has been made on Dr Davison's credit card and also that Leonora was in a hotel with a man shortly after the murders.

The proprietor of Café Noir identified Leonora from a photo as the woman who had been in the café on 3 November, ordered Moët Chandon and cheesecake and had left with a man. 'I remember her. She seemed strange, she kept looking out the door. She was tall and blonde. We don't have many people drinking champagne that early in the day and especially not Moët and especially not with cheesecake,' he laughed. 'What did she do?'

'We can't tell you,' said the younger detective, flipping his notebook shut. 'A crime's been committed, that's all we can say.'

Love and Marriage

Leonora was tall, beautiful and athletic. She played tennis, golf and squash. She painted, too. She was popular and had lots of friends. She was studying for an Arts degree, majoring in English Literature. Sam was a bit of a nerd. Brainy but pallid, skinny – a bit of a beanpole – bespectacled and serious: a medical student and upwardly mobile but boastful and always seeking approval. He was the kind of person who always had to take someone down to feel good about himself. Most other students regarded him as a loose cannon. His marks were spectacular, his social skills abysmal. From the start, as she later admitted in her testimony, Leonora saw Sam's role as being loving and supportive of her and to be the father of her children. She thought happy ever after was guaranteed. It was what she had been brought up to expect. It was the life path for a clever, beautiful Catholic girl raised in a close-knit Italian-Australian family. Her father owned a construction company and earned good money, so she grew up with an affluent middle-class lifestyle in Sydney. They even had a maid and Leonora grew up wearing designer clothes. Her younger brother Lorenzo (everyone called him Laurie) grew up to be an accountant. Her parents treated him like a Medici prince.

'Look!' she remembered her mother telling her with great excitement when she was eleven, 'I found a Dior tracksuit for you in a boutique. It's white – don't get it dirty.'

'Thanks, Mum,' she said, wondering how on earth she would not get it dirty.

Clearly it wasn't for playing sport, but for show. She took it to her bedroom to see how it looked. She decided she looked like a winner in it. A fair-haired winner who, naturally, looked good in a Dior tracksuit.

Her mother didn't have to do housework, so she was always going to gardening club or book club or attending charity events. Her name was Antonella: a name Leonora thought was so beautiful it was actually a perfect description of her mother. Antonella Morelli – it was almost a song. Her mother was a tall, slim brunette and stunningly beautiful with fantastic skin that went a shade like dark honey in summer.

Her father, Carlo, was good-looking too – fair-haired and blue-eyed. He called himself Carl and sometimes he told people his name was Charlie: it sounded so Australian, he said.

Leonora took after him, while Laurie was tall, dark and handsome. Always involved with some poor girl who was obsessed with him while he remained above it all, as a Medici prince would. Until he met Lee Roberts, a gorgeous girl with black hair cascading to her waist and a smile that could have powered an entire city. Then he was obsessed, and eventually married, in a huge society wedding at the biggest Catholic cathedral they could find.

Sam was also a Catholic, at least in theory, so in 1972 they had a big church wedding in St Luke's cathedral but the marriage was far from idyllic, even though the honeymoon in Fiji was heaven on earth as far as Leonora was concerned. They had spent their wedding night in a very expensive hotel, paid for by her parents and flown to Fiji the next day. The first time they had sex, Sam carefully inspected the sheet and there it was: the spot of blood that proved she had been a virgin. Leonora was proud of that spot but Sam acted slightly dismissive. He had deflowered a virgin, so that was one point ahead for him, and Leonora had kept the faith with what her mother and father and society at that time expected of her. She was not a slut; she had kept her part of the bargain. Every day in Fiji was spent having sex while the ocean waves rushed outside the window and then the night was spent the same way. They would lie half naked in the sun sipping cocktails and eating whichever delicacy the waiter had just carried over to them. All that marred her bliss was a case of what they called 'honeymoon cystitis', a bladder infection, as the Fijian doctor told her jovially. But a few antibiotics soon had her on the mend.

'Too much sex,' the doctor teased her as he wrote the prescription.

She blushed bright red and looked down at her hands. It was a whole new world and, in spite of the bladder infection, she liked it. She was a real woman now, with a man of her own.

Sam would not allow her to have a maid and told Leonora she had to do all the housework – the way his mother had while they struggled to survive on his factory worker father's wage. He was the first one in his family to go to university; being working-class among a lot of well-off people from upper middle-class families put the chip on his shoulder, and his feelings of inadequacy, the need to prove himself in every way, especially in bed, probably came from that. During courtship, Leonora had had her own money and her own car but Sam ended that once she was his wife. He took charge of everything and she simply had to do as she was told or there was trouble.

'You don't need that car. We can't afford it. We have to focus on getting me a medical degree – and then you can have a Porsche,' he told her, grinning while he kissed her and fondled her breasts.

She made no further protest about the car. Before they were married, he would take her to his room at the university. Then he would push her on to the bed and undress her for an extensive session of 'heavy petting', meaning he did everything but fuck her and then she had to use her hand to finish him off. Her mother and especially her father would have been livid if they had known. They trusted her to keep her virginity for her wedding night, which she did – technically.

'You look like a goddess,' he often told her as he climbed off the bed. One time even adding, 'You look like a heavenly body,' and grinning sexily while twisting her long blonde hair around his fingers and biting her neck.

When he said things like that, she was never sure if he was joking or not. Later, she realised that she had indeed looked like a goddess and he probably thought she was too good for him. Which explained his constant need throughout their marriage to belittle her and try to make her feel stupid and useless.

Within weeks of the wedding, Leonora was talking about divorce and so was Sam. A friend testified that only two weeks after the wedding Sam believed he had made a terrible mistake. But within a month Leonora was pregnant, so divorce became less and less of an option. There was no way Sam would accept being separated from his child. They simply had to soldier on. They were unprepared for a child in every way. Their first child, a fair-haired girl they called Clare, slept in a drawer for the first two months of her life, until Sam finally agreed to buy a bassinet. When Leonora went into labour with her second child (named Cecilia after Leonora's grandmother) Sam was working on an assignment, a vital paper for his medical degree, so she drove herself to the hospital.

'Don't worry,' she said, between contractions, 'I'll be fine. Just keep writing that assignment.'

He didn't even look up and mumbled, 'Great.'

Clare was asleep in her bassinet and Antonella was on her way to the house to look after her. Leonora struggled out to the car, forced herself into the driver's seat, her belly pressing on the wheel as she sped down the driveway and into the night. She was a loyal and supportive wife and tried to always see Sam's point of view. But she later told friends she was 'stupid' and 'gullible' and 'spineless' to put up with the things he said and did. It indicated a lack of self-esteem that had certainly never been evident before she married Sam.

The sexual revolution was in full swing but Leonora smugly thought that it never touched Sam or her. While others took the pill and tried free love, she thought they were having babies and preparing to be as upwardly mobile as possible. Materialism was their norm, not a scourge as the hippies believed. She was a bit arrogant and self-righteous. Sam was studying, and she thought he was working so hard that she felt she had no right to complain and immersed herself in her babies. Their third child, a boy, died two days after he was born but their lives were such a whirlwind of so many conflicting demands there was no time to really grieve. The baby had had a heart defect. A perfectly formed little boy with dark hair and slate grey eyes.

'We'll make another one,' Sam told her with no emotion, as if he was talking about a dropped cake.

She froze. He didn't even hug her. He went into his room to study, closing the door, and she sat at the kitchen table and couldn't even cry.

The doctor had told her to bind her breasts so her milk wouldn't come in. She got up from the chair and found the bandage she had bought at the pharmacy and bound her breasts. Then she went back to the chair. She wanted Sam to hold her, desperately needed him to do it but he was locked in his own world of study and ambition. Only at the funeral could she cry, looking at the small, white coffin as it was lowered in to the grave. On the headstone it would read, 'Callum Davison 5 June–7 June 1975' and there would be angels on either side of the stone. Angels with white wings, looking upwards.

And then Sam graduated and could start making money. Before long, he had joined a medical practice and they could finally get a house of their own. Later on, when the hate set in, and an Arctic wind began blowing in her direction, she would remember her wedding night as if it was something she had dreamed. She had run her hands up and down his back, she was too nervous to touch his butt, though she wanted to: he felt like silk and smelled like beer. He had drunk of lot of beer at the wedding reception but not enough to prevent him carrying out his marital duties on their wedding night. The smell of beer had been an aphrodisiac for her ever since. She was a virgin, so it hurt a bit at first but she loved him so much and loved what he did to her. He was sweet and gentle that night. So much hers that she could never imagine a time when he would not be. Her job, she testified in court, was to make him happy. If someone had told her a time would come when she would call him 'fag' to his face (because she knew that was the worst insult, in his eyes), she would have dismissed the idea as unthinkable.

Soon after Clare was born, Sam was having dinner in a restaurant with a twenty-something called Chiara. Leonora was at home with the baby, trying to establish a breastfeeding routine. She was frazzled and short-tempered a lot of the time. Sam gazed hungrily at Chiara's lovely face. They were having dinner by candlelight, and the flickering flame enhanced her alabaster skin and striking green eyes. He had always known that one woman was never going to be enough for him. He was clever, so it was easy to convince Leonora that he was working whenever he wanted a night with Chiara. Sometimes he was paged but not all that often. Then he would have to leave that lovely face and body in the hotel room bed and go to the hospital to deal with all kinds of medical emergencies. Once it was sorted out, he would return to Chiara, even if it was two in the morning. Sometimes her sleepy, love-drugged face made him kneel by the bed as if he was worshipping her. Then, even if he was tired, he would make love to her yet again. Leonora was so caught up with getting pregnant and having babies and working stacking shelves in a supermarket she never suspected a thing. Being a doctor was the perfect cover. When Chiara slept with her back to him, he would run his hands over her perfect little arse and kiss her all over the back until she woke and turned over so he could kiss her breasts, suck her nipples and enter her body. It wasn't love. It was just sex and it was wonderful, a luxury, while Leonora was as comfortable as an armchair and a natural breeder who would give him lots of children. He found this a natural state of affairs. Leonora adored him and would be faithful but he was a man and man was a hunter.

'You're so beautiful,' Chiara would whisper in his ear.

'No,' he would tell her, 'you're the beautiful one,' but of course it made his ego purr to be told this.

Chiara was blonde, like Leonora, not tall but perfectly built and as delicate as a piece of china. He bought her bracelets so he could enjoy looking at them on her slender wrists and green china cups that matched her eyes. He bought her a string of pearls on his credit card so he could enjoy looking at them around her slim, tanned throat. She was a lawyer and a tough little nut in many ways. Which is why she ended it when she found out he was married.

'You're married, aren't you?' she asked him on the phone, crying.

'My wife is a problem…'

'I don't want to know. I don't want to see you ever again.'

'Sweetie…'

'No, it's over.' The phone went dead.

He probably broke her heart but *c'est la vie*. He soon had another woman under his spell.

Going home after one of his trysts, Sam was always amazed at how bad Leonora looked since she had a baby. She was not fat but she was flabby, wore no make-up, hardly even bothered to comb her hair unless she was heading out to her job at the supermarket. She was usually asleep when he got home but sometimes she was up feeding the baby, or the baby was teething and would cry all night. She had shadows under her eyes. He left her to it. Put in earplugs and slept the sleep of the just. He had to be completely alert to deal with his patients and looking after the baby was her job.

Thrills on the Side

A year after that big cathedral wedding, Sam got adventurous. He had never had a threesome: for fear of failure to perform, though he never admitted it to himself. But when he was high on ecstasy, he thought he could manage. The drug made him even hornier than usual – to his amazement. It made him want two women or even more to have sex with. So he organised to have two prostitutes meet him in a hotel room. He pretended to know all about it, that he knew the rules: in fact, he had no idea how it was supposed to work but he was sure they did.

'Do you want us separately or at the same time?' the pretty blonde asked him. She was wearing short shorts and a tiny cotton top that revealed the tops of her generous, tanned breasts.

'Your tits are pretty,' he said.

'And the rest?' she grinned.

'It's all pretty.'

The brunette wasn't pretty, she was drop-dead gorgeous. Looked Latin – probably Italian or French genes – but as was probably usually the case with women in her profession, she also looked downtrodden and edgy. Insecure.

'We can do you together or one after the other,' the brunette offered.

'Together,' Sam told her.

He had ordered champagne, so now they toasted each other as if they were old friends and drank together. After the first glass, they all relaxed. The women undressed and so did he. Once on the bed, they went to work on him with great skill. One kissed him while the other took his erect penis in her mouth and used her tongue on the head to great effect. He couldn't see who was doing what. His eyes were closed and a blissful, sensual warmth started at the top of his head and spread slowly down his entire body. He opened his eyes and saw the brunette climbing on top of him. Her beautiful body seemed to glow in the darkness of the room as he watched a plane through the plate-glass window flying over, lights twinkling in the night sky. The brunette took his stiff penis in her hand, straddled him and put it in. Then she moved briskly back and forwards as the other girl continued to kiss him, exploring his mouth with her tongue. Pleasure flooded every part of his body. The brunette put her arms around him and held him tightly as she moved on top of him but he felt that embracing her would be wrong. He didn't know why.

He came and they lay down next to him, one on either side. The brunette was breathing fast, but not the blonde. He had paid for the night. After about thirty minutes' rest, he climbed on the blonde and fucked her. Her body was lean but soft as silk. She didn't come, although she was too professional to seem anything but thrilled. Soon after, he had his mouth between the brunette's legs and used his tongue to make her come. She seemed to try to avoid orgasm, he could feel her resisting, but then she relaxed, gave in and moaned with pleasure. He fell asleep. Napped for about an hour. When he woke, his first thought was that they would be gone and so would his wallet, but there they were, dozing on either side of him like obedient children. They took turns pleasuring him all night, except for when they both moved all over his body in unison like a conquering army. They had naps in between.

'How old are you?' he asked them.

'Eighteen,' said the blonde.

'Nineteen,' the brunette told him, smiling.

He supposed this was a good night for them. He was clean, good-looking and not violent (not to them: Leonora would tell another story) and he was paying them a lot of money. They seemed to be happy enough to spend the night with him but afterwards he thought, 'How would I know? How could I tell?' Their beautiful faces were opaque and gave nothing away. He had no idea what they were really thinking. What did it matter? It was a business transaction, after all.

After he left the hotel mid-morning, he went to see a movie: *Last Tango in Paris*. It seemed tame after what he had been doing, and Marlon Brando looked bored.

It was Ellen Brown who told Leonora about Sam and the prostitutes. A friend of a friend worked in reception at the hotel.

Leonora laughed out loud. 'That's just ridiculous!' she shouted angrily. 'He's working day and night to support our family and you think he's got the energy to take prostitutes to hotels. Ridiculous. And two of them at that. I don't know why anyone would tell such lies. I think it's jealousy.'

She couldn't be persuaded otherwise. She insisted it was just a case of mistaken identity. 'It doesn't matter what you say, Ellen. I'm not going to fight with you. I have too many real worries to get caught up in fantasy and gossip.'

Ellen hadn't been so concerned about Leonora since they were in high school together and Leonora had driven away boy after boy in her single-minded quest to remain a virgin for her wedding night. She often seemed mad in those days and there was a glimmer of madness in her eyes again. The truth was hammering at the door and Leonora was saying, 'Go away, I don't want any of that, thank you.' Ellen left thinking Leonora was losing the plot. She never trusted Sam after that and had to admit to herself that she had never liked him in any case and wished now that Leonora had never met him. She knew that the friend of a friend was right and this was going to mean real suffering for Leonora at some point.

After Ellen left, Leonora ate an entire packet of Tim Tams and made herself sick. Then the sickness became a migraine. She went to the bedroom and drew the curtains and pulled down the blinds; drifting in the dark like a species of deep water fish, as the pain tore through her head like a jackhammer.

The Sweet Smell of Success

By 1976, Leonora found herself in a five-bedroom house in Double Bay. Money had suddenly started rolling in. She thought, as she later testified, 'Everything was going to plan. Everything was going to be rosy.'

So she thought. In spite of their newfound affluence and the two young children, she was still working nights stacking shelves at a supermarket. They had taken on a lot of debt and Sam had very expensive tastes – tailor-made suits and the best wines for their new wine cellar. Leonora could only venture out in the prettiest and most expensive clothes. She had also discovered an appetite for jewellery that was hard to satisfy, so her wage was needed.

When Sam was eleven, his mother hired a nanny. It was just after his father had died; just months after the new baby, Caroline, was born and brought home. The nanny was a buxom, nineteen-year-old blonde from Norway, backpacking around Australia. Her name was Vilde. Sam couldn't take his eyes off her and often spied on her in her bedroom, watching her strip naked before she took a shower. Watching her dress to go out on dates with lucky boys. She was a glorious creature and always smelled of flowers, because she used a floral-scented perfume. The smell of freesias always reminded him of Vilde. She was his consolation for the loss of his father and being replaced by the baby. While watching her naked one afternoon, he suddenly realised his penis had become hard. It was the first time a woman had made it hard and when his mother suddenly appeared, he blushed fiercely, even though she didn't seem to notice anything.

'What are you doing?' she demanded. 'Where's Vilde? I need her to bath the baby. She's never around when I need her,' she grumbled, pushing back her unruly fair hair, drooping over her forehead in the heat, and disappearing up the hall to Vilde's room, where Sam knew she wasn't because he had been spying on her in the bathroom, peeping through the keyhole.

When Vilde came out of the bathroom, her face rosy and her lovely throat bare, Sam could only stare at her.

She patted his head. 'Hello, little man,' she said, in her low, accented voice and he blushed again and got hard again. Vilde noticed and giggled. 'Well, well, well, soon you'll be a big man, won't you?' she giggled again and went up the hall and then he heard his mother telling her to bath the baby.

She was his first blonde but he could only adore her from afar. The day she left, moving on to backpack her way to West Australia, she gave him a kiss on the cheek and made a prediction: 'When you grow up, the girls will be around you like bees around honey.' She obviously had the gift of prophecy.

In spite of the affluence and all the bright, shiny things Sam and Leonora could now buy, they still ended up in marriage counselling. Part of it involved writing letters to each other and giving them to the other person to read. Sam's letter admitted his failings as a husband but lacked depth or any true contrition.

Leonora's on the other hand was a *cri de coeur*, full of accusations and regrets, simplistic plans to fix things.

> You're so distant, so cold, so removed from me by work, by money and the children. There's no affection, sex is formulaic. I'm constantly anticipating disaster. I don't know exactly what. Just a doomy feeling. We don't even have a couch. If we could even just sit together and share our feelings, talk about our day. We aren't even physically close any more – or so rarely it doesn't count. And emotionally we're on different planets.

She had no idea how true that really was.

Having struggled so long to reach the future they dreamed of, it all seemed to be turning to ashes. But Leonora was a fighter. She would not give up – Sam belonged to her and he had made her his when he took her virginity on their wedding night. For her, those vows and the bond they created were unbreakable and yet she was trapped in domestic trivia and Sam was removed from her and absorbed with all his medical battles. Life and death battles she had no way of sharing. They were both bright people, but faced with the widening gulf between them, she could only watch helplessly as it widened into an abyss. Sam didn't mind the gulf, it protected his secret love life. So he retreated more and more into his work life (and, unbeknown to Leonora, his other women) and Leonora found comfort and self-esteem increasingly in her children, her clothes, her jewellery and going to social events, where she could play the trophy wife on Sam's arm. It didn't seem unfair to her that to pay for this lifestyle she was stacking shelves and sometimes working at night in a restaurant. She saw it as her duty.

Leonora had a lot of friends but they were all people she knew from the children's school or from the clubs she and Sam were in – golf clubs and tennis clubs. The closeness she longed for, the affection she needed from Sam, didn't exist. That area was just an icy nothingness at the centre of her life.

Various work colleagues gave differing opinions on Sam to the police when the murder first hit the headlines. One described him as 'A brilliant doctor. You see someone like him rarely. Incredible diagnostician. I would have trusted him with my life.' Another described him as 'Cold, cold, cold. A killer mind but unless he wanted or needed something from you he was cold as ice. I never liked him.' But it was Leonora's killer mind that the police were obsessed with. This killing was no random act as far as they were concerned – it was planned. She went there with a gun and she fired five shots.

Leonora's last child was born in 1979 – one of two boys she brought into the world. They called him Thomas, and he looked like Sam, although he had her blonde hair and not Sam's nut-brown hair. She got pregnant again seven months after his birth, her sixth pregnancy. Her doctor advised that the pregnancy could endanger her life, so the good Catholic girl had an abortion and had her tubes tied off to prevent any further pregnancies. Sam refused to have a vasectomy. Later on, she thought he was already making other plans that might have included another partner and future children. Paranoia perhaps, but it's not, as they say, paranoia when they're really out to get you.

Perhaps the real reason she had her tubes tied off was the one she gave in an interview just as the trial was beginning. Tom Perry was a tough and experienced journalist and he was researching a book that would be published after the verdict. Its working title was 'The Golden Couple'.

Sobbing, Leonora told Perry, 'I was like a single mother. Sam was never there. He was not only physically absent much of the time but emotionally absent all the time. Even during sex, I felt lonely.'

Sam loved skiing, so they went to Thredbo and later took vacations in Colorado in the US so that he could indulge his love of the sport. He bought a powerboat. The wine they bought for their cellar now was much more expensive. Their children went to the best private schools and Sam could now take the family on trips to Europe. They even took a cruise in the Caribbean. To the outside world, they seemed to be the golden couple of Perry's title, living a dream life – the perfect family. Leonora no longer worked in supermarkets or restaurants. She was high society now.

The woman in Sam's arms was not his wife. Just back from the Caribbean and very tanned, he was looking devastatingly handsome. The woman was a waitress in a coffee shop where he sometimes had breakfast on his way to work. She had waist-length black hair, hazel eyes and a glorious body. She was twenty-one, studying accountancy and working as a waitress to support herself through university. He kissed her passionately and held her tightly while his finger lightly stroked her clitoris. She moaned and kissed his chest. She was a real firecracker in bed and out. A lefty through and through, always talking about social justice and beating the feminist drum. He let her talk. He even pretended to agree sometimes because she looked so impossibly lovely when she got wound up. But he thought it was all nonsense. The world was the way it was. His kind got ahead, her kind got ahead and those who didn't were also-rans. He didn't care what happened to them. As for women: until they learned not to love men the way they did, they would never have justice. Look at Leonora. She could have done anything she wanted, but once she fell for him it was all thrown aside and now she had no idea who she was or what she wanted. She had become a cipher, a mumsy drone, as most of them did. He took hold of his penis and drove it into the girl. Her name was Kerry and her sweet pussy contracted as she writhed in pleasure. She made him crazy. He was with her for almost a year before he moved on to Daniella, a part-time model and actress with flaming red hair and dark brown eyes. Italian-Australian like Leonora but a very different person. Ambitious and a bit of a bitch, with just enough grit to be fascinating, but not enough to win an argument. He was only an amusement to her. She had plenty of other men. She lasted six months. A few years later, he heard she had married a member of parliament. He saw her on the news one night in a pale pink dress the exact colour of her nipples. He laughed at that. She smiled when she came and knew the entire 'tomorrow and tomorrow and tomorrow' speech from Macbeth. She once delivered it in a restaurant and earned a round of applause from the other patrons.

By the late seventies, the Davisons had a full-time housekeeper, Kate Ryan, and when Leonora became involved in working for several charities, she hired au pairs to look after the children. Sam was like a kid in a candy store with the au pairs and nearly got caught in flagrante delicto a couple of times but Leonora was oblivious to it all. He was skilled at hiding such things by then. Sam gave her thousands of dollars every month for household expenses and the children's needs and she also had credit cards which she used to buy expensive clothes for the dinner parties she gave and for the charity balls she attended.

In the early eighties, Leonora told an interviewer from a women's magazine doing an article on her charity work, 'Those who are fortunate must help those who are not.' She was wearing pearls and diamond earrings at the time.

In spite of the wealth, Sam was an angry man. He broke things and ripped a cupboard door off its hinges. When he came home angry from the hospital, Leonora would tell the children to stay out of his way and, above all, not to annoy him. The housekeeper testified under questioning in court that Sam was sometimes so angry that his sons were silent and fearful around him.

'What are you doing, you dolts?' he would scream at them. 'Settle down or you'll be sorry.' This was sometimes accompanied by him smacking them hard over the head with his hand. This was his response to them playing, arguing, rough housing – being normal boys, in other words.

Leonora never intervened for fear he would turn on her. She was angry too, throwing small pieces of furniture and scratching Sam's arms when he came home late, drunk and dismissive of her complaints. She was not getting sex by that time and she liked it and needed it, not that she would ever have admitted it to Sam – or anyone else. Though she did later, during the trial.

'He could turn it on and turn it off,' she said. 'He used it to punish me. If I wasn't good, I got no sweets.'

When Leonora was pregnant with her sixth child, the one the doctor advised her to abort, Sam got another woman pregnant. Her name was Alexa Tate, and her father was a conservative politician. She was sixteen. Alexa had flaxen hair and cornflower blue eyes. She stood about six feet tall with long, tanned, seemingly endless legs and a face like an angel. He wasn't surprised she was pregnant from one perspective, because he couldn't keep his hands off her and had sex with her in every possible position and whenever he could but that she wasn't on the pill surprised him hugely. Worse still, she told him she was in love with him and they would have to get married.

'You know I'm already married! I told you, you silly girl. How can I possibly marry you? I have responsibilities. I have a wife and I have children. It's completely out of the question.'

She put her angel head down and wept at this. But he knew he had to be firm. He was in grave danger: her father was a politician, a household name, and it would be splashed all over the papers if anyone got hold of it.

'You'll have to have an abortion,' he told her sternly and she cried as he was sure she had never cried before, at that. 'It's no use crying. We have to be practical,' he said, looking very much like a rat in a trap, which is what he was. 'I'm a doctor. I can't have any scandal attached to my name. You know that don't you, Dolly?' This was his nickname for her.

She sobbed a bit longer but then she got some toilet paper and vigorously blew her nose on it. 'Just give me some time to get used to the idea,' she pleaded.

But Sam was relentless. 'It has to be done as soon as possible. I can organise it. I know a gynaecologist who will do it. A top man. One of the best gynos in Australia.'

She gave a few more sobs.

'Think of your father. Think of the scandal. It might even get him turfed out of his seat. You know what the media's like.'

She did indeed. She had listened to her father ranting about them for years. Ever since she could remember, in fact. 'Yes. All right. You arrange it,' she said sorrowfully.

He wanted to put his arms around her and tell her she could have the child, that he would leave Leonora and do 'the right thing' but of course he did none of that.

A week later, the pregnancy was terminated but it was the beginning of the end for their relationship. If an affair with a sixteen-year-old schoolgirl could even be called that. She became resentful and one night full of booze she told him,

'I hate you! I hate you! Sometimes I feel like killing you, the way you killed our baby.'

He told her she was hysterical and she threw a bottle of champagne at his head. Blood trickled down his face and she started to laugh, pointing at him and falling on the couch. Then she vomited on the couch. That was pretty much the end of that. Even though she told her parents, there was not one word about it in the papers. The power of the politician, he thought, but he was never certain who put the frighteners on the media: he was just glad they had. If Leonora found out, he was sure she would leave him. She thought he was some kind of saint and no one would send their daughters to a doctor who got a sixteen-year-old pregnant.

Sam's eldest daughter testified at the trial that her father would sometimes kick the dog and swear at her mother. The façade they presented to the world was nothing like the truth but, in spite of all that, the younger daughter, Cecilia, testified that she believed they had a happy family and she never saw her mother cry. It seems never to have occurred to her that her mother might have cried alone, out of sight of them all.

In the late eighties, however, as the divorce grew ever more toxic, in a rare moment of self-reflection, Sam admitted to a work colleague that he had never been a loving husband to Leonora. That might explain Leonora's rage and frustration but not that final horrifying act of retribution. By the time that happened, Sam had turned Leonora's life into a living hell and she eventually saw only one way out. She knew nothing about the other women and his equally horrible treatment of some of them and Sam was as diligent and cunning as a spy in keeping it from her. He knew, prig and moralist that she was, that she would never understand his need for constantly changing sex partners, even though his contempt for the women who fulfilled his needs would have been very familiar to her.

Once he decided it was over and he was going to divorce Leonora, he still kept his secrets. For one thing, it made him feel superior to her, more powerful, and he also knew she would despise his inability to be faithful, something she had no trouble with at all. He had once screamed at her sarcastically during a fight that she was 'naturally virtuous'. She looked completely uncomprehending. She was always going to be a good Catholic girl: she couldn't help it. So of course she was virtuous. She couldn't see it as an insult or a complaint. Being virtuous was her duty as his wife and the mother of his children – in the same way her own mother had been. That was why she tolerated the intolerable and tried to fix it from her side when the only person who could fix it was Sam. Deep down inside, Sam knew she was in many ways a better person than he was and he hated her for it. It didn't make him want to be better, more like her. It made him want to destroy her because the idea that she was superior to him in any way was not to be endured.

A Night at the Opera

Sitting in the cell, Leonora thought about the night Sam had completely lost it. He had been out: he said he was going to the opera with another doctor, a male doctor he claimed. Leonora hated opera. Was it *The Barber of Seville*? She thought it probably was. He came home at one in the morning. He smelt of sex and some sweet, girlish perfume, possibly Daisy. Leonora had been waiting for him to come home. He changed and came out into the lounge room.

She was in a fierce rage and couldn't control herself so she flew at him like a demon and clawed his face and neck. 'You bastard! You shit! Who do you think you are? You've been with her, haven't you?'

'Been with her? Who her?' he laughed and sneered at her.

'You know who I mean, you pig! Susan Ross.'

He put his hand on his heart and said, 'I can assure you I haven't been with Susan Ross.'

His words made her feel as if she was falling, falling down an endless chute. It had to have been her. The alternative was simply too horrible for her to face. That there were others.

She was screaming at him when he suddenly punched her in the stomach as hard as he could and she sank to her knees, moaning, too hurt even to cry. Then he grabbed her by the hair and dragged her into the bedroom. He threw her at the bed from the doorway and she only just landed on it. She thought he was going to rape her but his urges had already been sated by the two women he had taken to the opera. He had sex with both of them high up in the gods on a very expensive private balcony. They were nurses. A redhead and a blonde.

Now, she realised, he was on something that night, cocaine or speed, because he then began to beat her with one hand while holding his hand over her mouth so the children couldn't hear her scream. He was mad with rage and very violent. He didn't stop hitting her and denigrating her in a soft, insinuating voice until around two in the morning. Then he left her lying there with a bloody mouth and a bruised face. He stormed out and she heard the car starting and the sound receding down the dark, silent street to God knew where. He was probably going to Susan Ross's flat in Paddington, she thought.

In pain, she managed to drag herself off the bed and into the en suite bathroom, where she cleaned her face and mouth up as best she could, took a shower and threw her nightie in the bin. It was completely ruined. She dried herself, watching in amazement as the bruises already began to show themselves from her face down her neck and all the way down to her lower legs, which he had kicked. She dried herself and put another nightie on and then she popped a Valium from the ones Sam had in the bathroom cabinet. She was shaking at first but the pill stopped the shakes and she eventually fell asleep.

The next day, Sam was nowhere to be seen and when she sat up in bed and tried to get up to get the children to school, she realised she could barely move. The sheets were bloody, so she tore them off the bed and hid them in a bin. There seemed to be no part of her body he hadn't beaten.

She phoned a friend, Valerie Danks, told her she was sick and asked her if she could take the four children to school with her two. She said she would, so then Leonora crawled to the bathroom and slapped makeup and concealer all over her face and neck and put a nice, deep pink lipstick on. She brushed her hair forward and put on a long dress with long sleeves. She took two painkillers and drank a cup of coffee. Thus fortified, she was able to get her children out of bed and give them breakfast. They could dress themselves and she checked that they all had money for tuckshop and had done their homework.

Clare knew something was very wrong but Leonora wouldn't tell her anything.

'I'm fine. I've got a sore throat, probably a throat infection,' she said, not looking her in the face for fear she would notice the damage she had covered.

'What was going on last night?' Clare asked her. 'I woke up and I could hear strange noises coming from your room.'

'Nothing was going on, what do you mean?' she stonewalled.

Clare shrugged and rolled her eyes. Her parents were infuriating.

Leonora didn't go out to the car, she just stood at the door and waved to Valerie. 'I don't want to give it to you,' she said in the raspy voice that was a result of having Sam's hands around her throat when he almost strangled her. It gave credibility to her story that she had a throat infection.

'You should go to the doctor. Get antibiotics,' Valerie shouted from the car.

'I'll see how I feel later,' she told her and waved to the children as the car backed down the driveway and drove away.

She didn't go to the police. And two days later, Sam was back, acting as if nothing had happened. The only sign that anything was wrong was that he gave her a diamond bracelet and matching earrings. She didn't speak to him for days but she took the diamonds. She had earned them. Had she gone to the police there would have been photographic evidence of his brutality.

A work colleague told the police that Sam had told him all about his night at the opera. Boasted about it. Sam had worn his cape. One of the rare occasions when he felt it was the right thing to wear. And it was very useful when one or other of the nurses was giving him oral sex. They could virtually disappear under his cape and get busy, with no one suspecting a thing. He 'had one of them on the floor of the balcony' as the opera raged on, full of high drama and high notes. Then he watched the opera for half an hour (a buxom brunette did a fine version of 'Una voce poco fa') and after that he had the other one sit on his knee, hidden in his cape, so he could 'do her from the back'. The noise of the opera drowned out her orgasmic cries. He would never see

The Barber of Seville the same way ever again, he told the colleague, laughing – he seemed not to see that its themes of deception and disguise fitted perfectly with his activities. So of course he was in high spirits when he walked through the door at home but there SHE was, flabby, angry and no fun at all. He beat her within an inch of her life, 'He said she deserved it for being such a mediocrity,' said the colleague. 'He not only wished he had never married her, he wished he had never met her.' He knew the end of his marriage was moving closer with every day, he told the colleague, and that meant he would have to marry Susan – because a man needed a wife, to keep the home fires burning and to raise his children.

This information was never used as evidence of spousal abuse at the trial. The whole story was so bizarre, so incredible, Rabinowitz thought, that the jury would dismiss it as nonsense. Leonora told the police about the beating when she was being questioned, but there were no photos, she didn't report it to the police at the time, and the cape, the threesome, were just too much for the average citizen to believe. Rabinowitz believed it, but he had been a lawyer for a long time.

Beautiful Susan

'She's beautiful,' Sam was saying.

Leonora turned to see who he was talking about. She had never heard him say that about anyone before. She couldn't see who he was referring to but later she asked him and he told her he was talking about a new receptionist in his medical building.

'Until then I had no idea she existed,' Leonora said, just before her trial began, while being interviewed by Tom Perry. This was in 1983 and Leonora would later say, more than once, 'Nineteen eighty-three was a knife slicing through my jugular.' Because Susan Ross, that was the receptionist's name, was her nemesis, figuratively and literally. Checking up on her, Leonora got the basic facts: she was a part-time model. She was twenty-five, five feet ten inches tall and incredibly beautiful. One of those people it was impossible to take a bad photo of. She had a lot of very white teeth, tanned smooth skin, masses of thick, slightly curly blonde hair and dazzling blue eyes, a perfect smile – and dimples when she smiled that smile. Even her feet were beautiful and she usually wore very pale pink nail polish on her toenails and favoured very elegant but slightly boho clothes. There was a photo of her on the brochure put out by the medical practice, wearing a pink and green kimono top and a leaf-green skirt. Standing behind her desk, smiling a dazzling smile with a phone to her ear. Her and her beauty, displayed tastefully.

Later, though, she found a photo in Sam's wallet of Susan in a white bikini taken in Hawaii on one of her holidays that came close to being an incitement to lust. Breasts spilling out of the bikini top and a minuscule triangle of white material for the bikini bottom which showcased her glorious tanned backside and tiny hips.

'Hawaii, the closest place to heaven on earth,' she had written on the back of the photo. Clear encouragement for Sam to prove that wasn't true.

'What's this?' Leonora yelled, throwing the photo in Sam's face.

He just picked the photo up and walked away without a word, a sardonic grin on his face.

Looking back, Leonora knew that she had made it all so easy for him. She took the kids away to a resort at the beach but Sam, as usual, had too much work to do to go.

'You know I'm working my arse off to keep this family afloat,' he bellowed. "I can't go to the bloody beach, not even for a single day.'

They were gone a month. And in that month Sam played the field as if he was a bachelor, even though Susan was his drug of choice.

The minute Leonora walked into the house, suitcase in hand, while the kids were rushing around trying to tell Sam about their trip, as he stared into space, she knew something had shifted. Like a cold breeze springing up on a warm day, something was off-kilter. The next day, during an extraordinary verbal attack as they drove to a birthday party up the north coast, Sam told her he hated their friends, told her she was old, overweight, dull and dumb. She would quote these words for years and no woman who heard them could ever again blame her for killing him, however much the act itself horrified them. While Leonora's looks were fading – in the classic phrase, she had let herself go – Sam, it seemed, was a late bloomer. His skinny frame had gained some pounds but it suited him. His hair was still thick, brown and glossy, his face unlined. He looked handsome and powerful and when he hired a secretary, Leonora was actually pleased that someone would help him with his workload. Until she found out it was Susan Ross. She had been promoted from receptionist. The news gave Leonora a strange sensation, as if a pair of hands were around her throat, squeezing.

Adding to her disquiet were reports from friends that Sam was seen in various places around town with the twenty-five-year-old Susan.

Susan was Catholic too, but she had none of Leonora's hang-ups. None of her inhibitions in bed. She was looking forward to having a big family and the father of choice was Sam. Susan had a wild side and went for what she wanted in a way that was unthinkable to Leonora; who found her suspicions confirmed when she saw the large office Susan Ross occupied and found out that she was being paid a salary of $50,000 a year – unheard of for a secretary at the time. She couldn't even type accurately and now she was being paid a large salary to be with Sam on a daily basis. Things soon came to a head.

'You're having an affair with Susan Ross,' she told him. It wasn't a question.

Cornered and feeling threatened Sam lashed out. 'You're crazy. You're delusional. I am not having an affair with my secretary. She's just my secretary and nothing else.'

Leonora begged to differ. 'Get rid of her. You've got a month. Get rid of her or get out of my house.'

To that, Sam replied, 'If you don't like things around here, you can get out. Because this house is not yours, it's mine.'

This was not strictly true but it was obvious that Sam intended to behave as if it was.

Testifying at her trial, Leonora was baffled, or said she was. 'I told him I couldn't understand why he was unhappy. He had a beautiful home, lots of money, healthy kids, anything he wanted was his. What else could he possibly want?'

She was being disingenuous. The thing he could possibly want was the young, taut body of Susan and her beautiful young face – and they both knew it. There were the others, too. Those lovely, willing girls Leonora didn't know anything about. Sam was a beauty addict; that was why he couldn't leave his children. The most beautiful possessions of all.

After the fight over Susan Ross, Sam arrived home one afternoon driving a red sports car that had midlife crisis written all over it. It was a Porsche Carrera and it cost hundreds of thousands of dollars. They could afford it but that wasn't the point. The thought of Susan Ross's shapely buttocks resting on the white leather seats made Leonora so enraged she got a migraine and had to lie in the dark for two days. Something had to give and on her thirty-eighth birthday, it did.

Now that it was all out in the open (or Leonora thought it was), Sam came home even later every night. He ignored her complaints and treated her with contempt. Then on her thirty-eighth birthday she organised a fancy dinner at home for him, her and their children. He didn't arrive in time for dinner, a deliberate snub, but Leonora put a good face on things for the children and tried to pretend everything was fine. Inside, though, she was devastated – and angry. After the kids went to bed and Sam had slouched off with a smarmy grin on his face to the bedroom they no longer shared, she sat up drinking, even though she wasn't a drinker and couldn't handle large amounts of alcohol. Around midnight, she went to the bathroom and swallowed every sedative in the bathroom cabinet, then she cut her wrists.

She woke to daylight and Sam saying her name and swearing. He asked her how she could do this to the kids – and to him. She listened in disbelief as he put all the blame for everything on her.

'You stupid bitch. You could have died: all that saved you is that you vomited. One of the children could have found you. You're a selfish monster,' he raged at her.

'And you're not? Think of what you're doing to the children. Playing around with that bloody woman. That homewrecker…'

'I'm not doing anything to the children. That's all in your crazy head.'

'You're lying! I know what's going on.'

The cuts on her wrists weren't life-threatening and Sam was a doctor. He bandaged her wrists and assessed her medically. She was in no danger, the pills she took only knocked her out but couldn't kill her. She hadn't swallowed enough of them before she passed out.

'You're having a breakdown,' he told her.

'Is that your medical opinion?' she sneered groggily.

'You're imagining this affair with Susan Ross. You're losing touch with reality,' he asserted. He was brisk and professional. He could have been talking to a patient.

'You bastard. We both know I'm right,' she told him wearily. 'How long do you think you can go on pretending like this?'

He didn't answer and soon after left in his red sports car.

Two weeks later, it was Sam's thirty-ninth birthday and following advice from a friend ('Show him you can be unpredictable,' she had told her), Leonora decided to go to his office and surprise him. She took a bottle of champagne and an ice bucket with her.

On arrival at the office, it was clear Susan Ross had beaten her to it. The remains of a chocolate cheesecake sat on a table in the office kitchenette. Sam had bought a refrigerator and a stereo system for his office. There was an empty bottle of wine and two wine glasses but no sign of Sam or Susan. A receptionist told her they had left around ten a.m.

Something inside her broke loose. Like a cartoon sprite bent on evil, she dumped the champagne in a bin and threw the ice bucket across Susan's office and watched it bounce off the spotless white walls. Longing to damage something, she headed out to her car and took off with a squeal of tyres. How she managed to drive home without wrecking the car, was, she thought later, a mystery. Sobbing hysterically and blinded by tears, she roared along the highway not caring if she lived or died. She was raving by the time she reached the house, completely out of control. In contrast to how she was by the time she fired the gun. Icy calm, with her finger on the trigger, firing again and again.

After leaving Susan asleep in the hotel room where they had birthday sex (he had planted a kiss on her silky shoulder in farewell), Sam jumped in his car and went to a rendezvous with another woman. Kathy was dark-haired, tall, lithe as a panther with perfect olive skin and a generous mouth that didn't quite meet over her slight overbite. Her teeth were incredibly white. They were in her beachfront unit at Bondi.

The waves crashed outside as he pulled her on to the bed and clamped his mouth on to her beautiful, large breasts with their caramel-coloured nipples. He kissed, he sucked and she wrapped her legs around him and rubbed her pussy up and down his leg. Susan had only whetted his appetite. No woman could ever satisfy him. As Kathy bucked and moaned in orgasm, he bit her neck ever so gently.

'Was that nice?' he whispered. He always liked applause after a performance.

But her only reply was an exhalation and some passionate, mumbled words he couldn't understand.

The children were at school, Leonora could take her time. She walked, full of purpose, to the master bedroom, threw the doors of the clothes cupboard open in a dramatic gesture worthy of a movie queen. She even wished she had a video camera to record what she was going to do. But who would she show it to? Sam? The children? Herself? She grabbed as many of his tailor-made suits as she could and dropped them on the ground in the middle of the yard; pouring kerosene over them and setting them alight. She didn't burn the cape or the top hat. Something she regretted later.

Sam eventually came home, full of boozy cheer and smelling of expensive perfume. In spite of that, he still claimed there was no affair and Leonora's screaming had no effect on him.

He surveyed the ruin of his suits in the backyard with equanimity with their horrified children at his side. 'See?' his face seemed to say. 'Your mother's a lunatic and I am the innocent victim.'

Then he ordered more suits. The only beneficiary was his tailor.

After that, she started a campaign to make herself more attractive to him. She got thin. She changed her hairstyle and grew it longer, the way it was when they married. She went to a doctor and had her wrinkles erased. She dropped out of her society things and stayed home. Surely if she was perfect he would love her again?

But Sam was in love with Susan and was a cheat by nature and no makeover would change that, even though he continued to deny that Susan was anything but his secretary. Sam had a fine mind and when he decided to use it against her, she was helpless. His denial of any impropriety with Susan was so that he could seem beyond reproach come the divorce and also give him time to shift his assets into safe havens. His friend Kevin was more than happy to help, after Sam spun him a horror story about Leonora and put all the blame on her. He moved some real estate and shares into Kevin's name.

Kevin told a friend who testified about it in court that he believed Sam's gaslighting of Leonora was carefully planned and well thought out. He wanted to so unbalance her that she would agree to spend time in a psych ward in a hospital. That would discredit anything she said about him, even with her own children.

It was probably because of that that her eldest daughter Clare told the court that her father was trying to take care of them but her mother was destroying all of their lives. Leonora went on believing Sam had a midlife crisis and ignoring his malevolence towards her until it was much too late. It only confirmed her in that belief when she watched several of her women friends go through what she was enduring. She told Tom Perry in an interview a couple of weeks before her trial began that 'Male midlife crises were common in my circle and led to several divorces.'

No matter how many times friends told her they saw Sam and Susan in restaurants, Sam denied everything. They were even spotted coming out of a hotel holding hands. Sam was sure Susan would go on believing him because he knew she still loved him – and he cynically used this against her while he moved as many assets as he could out of her reach and set himself up as the responsible parent for when he went for full custody of the children. Using the excuse that the house had to be repaired and renovated before it could be sold, Sam moved Leonora and the children into another rented five-bedroom house in Rose Bay. But by the time he turned forty, he'd had enough. He left in the red sports car with the chequebook and the credit cards.

'You're a cliché,' Leonora told him bitterly. 'You're a joke.'

Even at that stage, she believed he was going through a midlife crisis and would get over Susan Ross. He let her think it; it was yet more proof that she was delusional and wilfully blind to the reality of their relationship.

Foreign Flesh/House Cleaning

For Leonora, there was nothing quite like housecleaning to give her that virginal, purified feeling. She was well aware that the first use of the word 'slut' was not directed at women who were too free and easy with sex, but at women who didn't clean their houses, who let the house work go. Presumably they did this so they could spend time with their lovers but the complete meaning of the word was to some extent lost in time.

When the urge to clean came over her, Leonora was helpless: she could not resist it. She would give the housekeeper the day off. She didn't want her hanging around trying to meddle. When she had the urge to clean, she wanted to do it all herself, with no interference and no help. She lined up her weapons: the mop, the broom, the vacuum cleaner, the cleaning cloths (she preferred Chux), the furniture polish and the special polishing cloth made of cotton, the orange cleanser to be sprayed around the bathroom and on the stove and the kitchen benches. The special blue cleaning cloth that attached via Velcro to the top of the sweeper that made her hallway sparkle like a diamond. All the little scrubbers that she used for the really tough dirt and stains.

Once again, the word 'scrubber' was one used to describe cleaning women, women who cleaned houses. Now it was used in some places to describe a working-class slut, so all these words had a beautiful symmetry but all were slurs directed at women for doing or not doing housework. Leonora didn't care that she was sublimating her sex urges into housework. The physical exertion, the thin sheen of sweat over her entire body mimicked the sweaty work that was sex and it satisfied her: being virtuous and not sinful in any way, there was no guilt and it made her feel like the good girl her mother had always told her she was.

But for Sam there was only the hunt for the perfect cunt. Nothing else had any real meaning in his life. Not even his profession. He could appreciate a woman as a person – at least some women – but nothing a woman would ever do could replace that magical organ between her legs that gave him a pleasure nothing else came close to replicating. No genius, no gift a woman had, impressed him as much as that moment when they parted their legs and he was allowed to enter that warm, wet paradise he thought about most of the time. Even when he was discussing palliative care with the relative of someone who was dying of cancer, he was thinking about cunts and how exquisitely pleasurable that first moment of entering one of them was. It probably meant he was a bad person but he didn't care about that. He was who he was.

While Leonora set up her weapons in her fight against dirt and slovenliness, Sam was meeting a girl for lunch – and sex, of course. He preferred a girl who hadn't showered. He was unhygienic to a fault and would often prevent a woman he had lusted after for weeks from showering.

'No, no,' he would tell them. 'Don't shower. I want you sweaty,' and he could have added 'smelly' but he had to keep some kind of decorum going or he would be seen as just plain crude instead of daring and sexy. His lack of hygiene during sex was in some ways a holiday from the rigorous hygiene imposed on him as a doctor.

Leonora began with the bathroom. She liked nothing better than making the toilet shine and sparkle and smell good. When she had finished with it, it gleamed as if it had just been installed. Then on to the tiles around the bathtub and shower. The orange spray and the scrubbers were put to use until she could see her face in the shining white tiles. Then the mop was used to clean the floor and the floor of the shower cubicle. They gleamed. The taps were all polished, the mirror was cleansed of every bit of toothpaste and until every smear disappeared. Perfect. Out came the special blue cleaning cloth that made the wooden floor shine like new. Then the other cloths were used to clean the walls. Then the vacumn cleaner picked up every trace of cotton, hair and bits of fluff. She wiped sweat from her brow. Into the kitchen. The white bench tops were scrubbed until every mark and any trace of dirt was gone. The stove was scrubbed until it was blindingly white. She even wiped the kettle and the coffee machine until they were absolutely clean. Out on to the deck and she used the special blue cloth to wipe every bit of dirt and every leaf off it too. She was sweaty but she felt good. All that remained was to polish the furniture and remove every bit of dust. She polished vigorously. The need for sex, the need to be held was gone and she put all the cleaning weapons away and settled down with a glass of wine to watch a movie.

It was muggy in the hotel room in spite of the airconditioning and the woman Sam was on top of was sweaty and slippery – but he loved it. The more sweaty she was, the more he had to struggle to stay on top of her, the more he loved it. She was giggling as he slipped and slid but she loved it as much as he did. Her name was Rachel, she was from Poland and had only been in Australia six months but spoke perfect English. She had just turned twenty and she was blonde and curvaceous with the most beautiful breasts he had ever seen. They were slightly red from where he had squeezed and sucked them but she had only made little moans of pleasure while he worked away. Now he was inside of her, the place where he always wanted to be and she was tight and wet and moved underneath him while her hands cupped his buttocks.

'You have a beautiful arse,' she told him breathlessly.

'So do you,' he said, pushing into her and even putting his feet on the floor so he could push harder.

'Ooooooooh. Ooooooh Gooooooood!' she moaned. 'Oh God. Oh God.'

He kissed her like a madman and she bit his face.

'Settle down, sweetie! Don't chew my face off,' he said, laughing.

'I won't. I promise,' she gasped caressing his chest, his nipples, his arse and then having a long orgasm. 'Ooooooooooh, oooooooooh, oooooooooooh,' she moaned.

He would be seeing her again. She was almost as good as Susan.

Leonora was slumped on the couch in a frumpy tracksuit watching *Double Indemnity* and there was a certain amount of irony in that. She was on her third glass of wine and hating adulterers one and all. Fred MacMurray got what he deserved, the moron.

Her husband was sleeping with a beautiful blonde by his side, and he was just waiting for the chance to get hard again. At two, he would have to go back to work, so he could only have sex twice. More than that and he would be the walking wounded all afternoon.

That Certain Something

Sam grew greedy. Soon after he met Susan, he decided he needed even more pleasure and that ecstasy would do it for him. He had no reason to do it, he just wanted to. He knew it heightened sexual pleasure – he had taken it before. But no one explained to him that it could have side effects.

He had arranged to meet a stunning girl in a hotel about a month after he started using the drug. She was black. Her name was Alice Adisa, she was eighteen and she was a very classy dresser. That day, she was wearing a beautiful red coat with glossy square buttons and a tight black skirt. Though African by birth, she had grown up in Australia, so she had an Australian accent. She told him she was planning to become a model, preferably a supermodel. He found her in a magazine, advertising her beauty and promoting herself as a model. Fabulous photos of her taken by a professional photographer spread over four pages; posing in high fashion garments. She was gorgeous. With a little detective work, he tracked her down. It wasn't easy and she didn't want to go out to dinner.

'I can't eat restaurant food and model,' she told him. 'I'm going to Paris soon.'

She had suggested they meet in a hotel and had chosen the hotel. She towered over Sam and was whip thin with an exquisite African face and hair cut very short, close to her head. When she took her clothes off, he thought her body looked like a work of art, like a sculpture. He ran his hands over her velvety skin and kissed her.

'I don't love you,' she said briskly. 'This is just sex. Some guys get clingy.'

Sam laughed in disbelief. 'You're sweet, but I don't need you to love me, just to make love to me.'

'Oh,' she said and smiled, flashing blindingly white teeth. 'Okay.'

Sam was quickly naked too, and then they were on the bed. He felt the heightened pleasure, he certainly did. It flamed through his body like a fire that caused pleasure instead of pain. She wrapped her long slender arms around him and wound her legs around him. But in spite of the fierce pleasure he was feeling, his penis stayed as limp as a strand of cooked spaghetti. It soon became clear that he was not going to rise to the occasion.

'This has never happened before,' he babbled, completely amazed at this turn of events.

Alice looked equally amazed. 'Don't you like me?' she asked, looking hurt.

'What? No! I like you, absolutely, you're gorgeous,' he told her, flustered.

'Should I suck?' she inquired.

Sam was prepared to try anything and it made sense that having this goddess suck his cock would make him ramrod stiff. She bent her lovely head and put her mouth around his member; but it was limp and it stayed limp no matter what she did.

'It's okay,' he said, expertly flipping her on her back and spreading her legs. 'Let's try this.'

He then used his tongue to give her an orgasm. At least he could do that. But there was no hope his penis was going to get hard. Watching her go off was lovely and very pleasurable but it was as if he loved the entire world and she was just a representative of that: it didn't seem to have much to do with him. He had never felt so disconnected from a woman and yet at the same time so connected to everything. She was kissing his chest and licking his nipples.

'That was beautiful,' she said.

'You're beautiful,' he told her gently, 'but maybe you should go now. I have your number, I'll call you next week and we'll try again.'

'Okay,' she smiled, all glowy and post-orgasmic but looking slightly baffled. 'You'll call me?'

'I will. Definitely,' he said, kissing her.

He watched her dress, cursing his penis. How could this happen? She gave him one last brilliant smile as she completed dressing and then she slipped out the door with a flirty wave of her fingers. He went to the window and watched her red coat and her long legs as she was getting into a yellow cab in front of the hotel. He was distraught over what had happened – or had not happened.

He went to the nightstand, picked up the phone and called his little, rat-faced dealer.

'Did you sell me the right stuff?' he asked him.

'Whaddya mean, dude?' the rough voice came down the phone, full of suspicion and, yes, no denying it, threat. These types became aggressive very quickly. 'Of course it was the right stuff. It was Molly, that's all. Not cut with anything. What's the problem?'

'Molly?'

'That's what they call it. It's a fuckin' nickname…'

'All I know is, I was just with a gorgeous woman and my penis stayed limp. Molly seems to be a bit of bitch.'

Ratface was laughing. 'Yeah, that can happen. Didn't you know that?'

'No, I didn't and you didn't tell me. Defeats the purpose, doesn't it?'

'Let the buyer beware,' said the dealer who was a half-educated smart-arse among other things.

'How long will it take to wear off? It will wear off, won't it?' Sam asked in a panicky voice.

'Sure. You haven't been taking it long, have you?'

'About a month – this time around.'

'I wouldn't worry. It's random. It may never happen again.'

Exasperated, Sam was about to hang up on him but he hesitated. A few weeks until he could have Alice again – damn that capricious bloody drug. He would have to wait because he would never subject himself to such humiliation again. That meant Susan and even Leonora were off limits too.

'A small dose of Viagra will do the trick if that happens,' the dealer told him in a helpful, medical-type voice. 'About a third of a tablet will be enough.'

'Viagra?'

'I thought you were a doctor,' said the smart-arse.

'How do you…? I am a doctor but I'm not a drug addict.'

'Aren't ya?' sneered Ratty.

'No, I'm not!' he shouted. And then he did hang up on him. Rat-faced freak. Nothing to do now but go home to Leonora. A huge wave of depression swept over him at the thought. Even more so, since he couldn't even have sex with her. Now he had to get some Viagra and Ratface probably sold that too. What a disaster.

That certain something, he was thinking. Why marry Susan? Why her? In moments of introspection, he asked himself this question. Of all the women he had slept with, why would he choose to marry Susan? He knew why he married Leonora. He was inexperienced in actual relationships with women and didn't see the warning signs until it was too late. But why Susan? Of course he needed someone to run his house and care for the children but in fact those needs were already covered by the housekeeper he had hired and the nannies he employed from time to time. No. It was more than that. It was, of course, that she was a fabulous animal in bed and incredibly beautiful. He wanted her for his own. He wanted her to have his name. He wanted her in his bed, in his house, in his car as proof that he was worth something himself. She was a trophy, of course, but it was more than that, too. She was the only woman who had ever really asserted herself with him. She took no shit from him because she was strong and tough and clever. She was his match, in every way.

Leonora had never been anything but compliant and it was boring. She bored him in bed too, even though he knew from the start that she was crazy about him. Her lack of experience meant he had to teach her everything and she was a poor student in the amatory arts. Making babies was far more thrilling to her than making love. He was sure the only time she ever really felt like sex was when she was ovulating. She was probably one of those women who ovulated when she came, too, thus her success at childbearing. He didn't blame her for his infidelities: that's just how he was, but Susan was truly gifted in the sack, knew her worth and was a bit of a bitch – all of that increased her marriageability.

Sam didn't believe in love, the romantic kind. To him, that was just a myth to trap women. Leonora believed in it passionately. That was her mistake.

The Art of War

February 1985 saw Sam moving out of the Double Bay house they were selling. Leonora demanded to know what she and the children were supposed to do. How would they survive? He had the chequebook, the credit cards and control of the bank accounts. He told her he needed space. That stupid cliché, she raged to herself. It was not about another woman, he told her. How stupid did he really think she was? Very, if this crap was anything to go by.

Leonora decided that whether it was about another woman or not, Sam needed a dose of reality. So when her oldest daughter annoyed her and fought one time too many with her sister, she drove her over to the new house Sam had bought and dumped her on his doorstep. Soon, her younger brother followed and eventually all of the children were living with Sam.

Once again, she had played into his hands. Bad Mother was added to the list of her sins and failings. She couldn't have been more helpful to his plans to go for full custody. Worst of all, Sam simply hired nannies and coped admirably with the children. They felt more secure with him because he was stronger than her and didn't have moods, didn't fall apart. Leonora was becoming a basket case and the children knew it. But her plan to make him see how much she contributed to the family backfired. Instead of Sam suddenly understanding how much she did for both him and the children, he found he could manage perfectly well without her.

He became the caring father, coming home earlier than usual at night so he could have dinner with his children. This had never been a major concern of his in the past. At first, Leonora coped reasonably well; turning up with groceries when the children told her the cupboard was bare and making sure they got to ballet or sports they were involved in. Sam let her do as she pleased and this arrangement continued for a while. Until a tremendous rage started to build in Leonora. It was now impossible for even her to believe his lies about his affair with Susan Ross, since she was at Sam's house every weekend. As the rage set in, Leonora began to throw tantrums. During one of them, she almost destroyed Sam's bedroom. She smashed a phone, put a hole in a wall and broke a couple of mirrors. A month later, she found sitting on Sam's kitchen bench a cream pie that Susan had made, and smeared it all over Sam's bedroom. The bedroom was the main focus of her rage, because it was where he slept with Susan on the weekends.

Turning to the police for help, Sam discovered that with Leonora's name on the deed to the house, she could do whatever she wanted. Sam's only recourse was to sell that house and buy one with only his name on the deed. As soon as the house Leonora was living in sold, he put a deposit on another house that cost half a million dollars and her name was not on the deed. It was a house Leonora had chosen and she soon began renovating. In time, Sam bought the house in Banksia Avenue too. The house where he and Susan would be murdered; but he had no thought of anything like that. He never really felt afraid of Leonora. To him, she was a figure of fun.

Leonora put in a volleyball court for the children to use and she was firmly convinced that the family would reunite and live in the house together.

But in March Sam filed for divorce. He made arrangements he probably thought were fair: $9,000 a month for Leonora's expenses. He would also continue to pay her insurance and the fees she needed for her club memberships and the cost of her involvement in charities. He wanted full custody and was willing to play dirty to get it. He told the Family Law Court that Leonora was mentally unstable and could not care for the children.

Leonora had led a sheltered life but once a woman neighbour reminded her about the word 'cunt', she used it freely and monotonously to describe Susan Ross. She also claimed that she was enraged that her children's Catholic morals were being compromised by exposure to an adulterous relationship – but she called Sam 'fuckhead' in front of those same children. Later, she claimed that what he was doing to her was completely monstrous and immoral and calling him and his mistress names was a mere nothing next to it.

When Leonora told Sam about her moral problems with his relationship with Susan, things quickly became violent. As she testified in court, 'That happened because he wanted to put me in a mental institution. He told me so. He provoked me as much as he could. He knew if he shoved me I would shove back – or if he hit me – so he did.'

And the name calling wasn't all on one side. Her youngest daughter Cecilia testified in court that Sam and Susan referred to Leonora as a fat, disgusting beast, an out of control bitch, even a bitch on heat.

And things had reached the point where Sam didn't want to see Leonora at all. 'I don't want to talk to her. Don't want to see her, can't stand the sound of her voice,' he told his children.

The Family Court decreed that Leonora could only go to Sam's house to pick up the children for mandated visits. Otherwise, she was to stay away from him and the house. Soon, Sam was living with the children and Susan in one house and Leonora was living alone in the house Sam bought her. She was still obsessed with Sam and had fantasies of emasculating him, telling one female friend, while in her cups, that she should shoot his balls off. In court, she denied she ever said it.

It was a measure of the dark place Leonora was in that when she was told that the now fully renovated house where they had raised their children had been sold, without her consent, she responded violently, even crazily. It was a warning of what was to come. She was at one of her dinner parties when she got a call from Sam's lawyer telling her that the Double Bay house had been sold.

'That bastard!' she howled into the phone.

She had known it was coming but the finality of it was too much for her. She had been drinking and now she went into full grief mode, howling like a banshee with tears running down her face. She left the dinner party, grabbed her handbag in the hall and drove off in her car, tyres squealing. That was pretty much how she drove now; even just taking off from a green light she made the tyres squeal. Sometimes she felt like an adolescent boy – full of hormones but denied sex and therefore relief. She wandered lonely and sex mad from day to day, crisis to crisis. She sped to Banksia Drive, raging to herself about the sale of the house, but Sam wasn't there.

Her daughter Cecilia was there and she later described her mother as 'Pale as a ghost with eyes that were unfocused.' Holding back tears, she told the court that her mother looked 'deranged'. It was hardly surprising that in this state, unable to talk to Sam and plunged into despair that this link with Sam and their life together had been snatched away, she drove to the Double Bay house, sold but presently unoccupied, and tried to set it on fire.

'Take that,' she snarled, laughing and sprinkling the contents of a petrol can around the front door. Of course she knew nothing about arson so her incendiary outburst caused only minor damage and fizzled out on the thick carpet on the stairs. Sam was the one she had always taken her troubles to and underneath all that rage she still loved him and suspected that she always would. But at this moment of crisis, she couldn't talk to him.

Then she drove back to the Banksia Avenue house determined to make Sam talk to her. Somehow that translated in her scrambled brain, full of toxic and conflicting emotions, into her driving her car into the entrance to the house, smashing the door in and damaging the brickwork around it. She would get Daddy's attention, one way or another.

Sam had been phoned and told what was going on and was now at the house to witness the mayhem. 'Stop this, you crazy bitch!' he shouted at Leonora. At some point, he might have felt that his plan to drive her crazy was working all too well.

Clare grabbed her younger brother and ran out into the backyard while Sam raced to the door, or what was left of it. Later testifying in court, Leonora said simply, by way of explanation, 'He treated me like dirt. There was no respect. He wanted me dead.'

When Sam tried to pull her out of the car, she produced a large knife. She carried it in her handbag at all times. In her enraged condition, it was a dangerous habit. Cecilia now watched her parents wrestling on the front lawn while Clare tried to separate them. She was flung aside, which was fortunate, because she could have been accidentally stabbed. Then Sam delivered a right hook to Leonora's jaw and she fell over backwards, knife in hand.

Eventually, the police arrived; Leonora had been disarmed. Cecilia told the court it made her cry to see her mother's 'blank eyes' as she sat handcuffed in the back of the police car. Even worse, as she stood there crying, her mother stuck her tongue out at her, like a wilful child.

Leonora told her lawyer, but not in court, that she did not regret ramming the house with her car.

'If I did it again, I'd do it with more planning. I was acting out of anger and my efficiency was affected. Sam took everything. Half of that house he sold was mine. I just couldn't process the fact that he had taken it too.'

Her lawyer pretended he had heard nothing and went on to other matters. Sam hired security guards to keep Leonora away from him and the children and, of course, the house. Susan had nightmares where she woke and the house was on fire.

'Nothing he did was not carefully calculated,' Leonora testified. 'I, on the other hand, was a travelling circus. For one night only!' she exclaimed, spreading her arms wide.

Some of the jurors looked sad, others curled their lips and seemed eager to pass sentence there and then.

'Getting rid of properties, not paying taxes, not paying credit cards. It was all calculated to play down how rich he was. I had seen other men in our circle do this, so I knew the process. Sam was merciless and relentless in protecting his wealth but he treated me, the mother of his children, as worthless, expendable. Yet I was the crazy one, according to him.'

Leonora was now divorced and Sam had full custody of their children. It wasn't difficult for him to do. Leonora's crazy behaviour and the obscene messages she left on Sam's answering machine meant a Family Court judge felt he had no choice but to protect the children from their mother, who was now seen as a clear and present danger – a threat to their physical and mental well-being.

Days of Rage and Compulsion

After the divorce, Leonora became a compulsive eater and spender. She could always find food, usually the worst kind, but money was another thing. Even when the court awarded her $16,000 a month, she wasn't satisfied. She pointed out that Sam earned around two million dollars in 1986, the only year she had been able to find his tax return for. She could only guess at what he was currently earning but knew it was a lot more. She had worked at night, even when she was pregnant, even when she had young children to care for, so that he could do the study that put him in a position to earn that kind of money. She thought she deserved at least $50,000 a month and was prepared to fight hard to get it. The truth was that she would have happily lived with Sam in a tiny flat if he would love her again, but she knew he couldn't and wouldn't and that left a hole inside her heart that was impossible to fill, with money, food or anything else. The court had mandated $192,000 a year as reasonable but Leonora could not be satisfied because all she really wanted was Sam and her family intact again. She had been high maintenance for years and was incapable of changing, spending huge sums on clothing which she always bought in a size that used to fit her but no longer did. So the clothes hung in her cupboard with the price tags still on them, unworn. Her weight had ballooned.

While Leonora ate herself huge and spent money on clothes she could never wear, Sam was still on the prowl. He found a girl standing outside a pub trying to phone a cab and soon lured her into his car. She was wild as the west wind. A tiny thing with dark brown hair, blue eyes and thick black eyelashes. She clung to him in bed like a frightened child. Sam didn't really like it. He liked his playmates to be strong and independent. She told him she was eighteen but he thought she was probably sixteen. She sold clothes in a boutique in Double Bay that a friend of her mother's owned and was always dressed as if she was going to a movie premiere and would have to walk the red carpet. Silken minidresses and six-inch heels and a geisha-white face and very red lips. She had simply refused to go to school any longer, so her mother told her she had to get a job. She smelled of chewing gum and cigarettes and Chanel Number 19.

She was so young he had to teach her everything. She had never had an orgasm with a man and had no idea how to achieve one apart from masturbating. Lots of sex with various partners but no orgasms, that had been her experience until then. Soon, he had her moaning under him, and on top of him. Watching her moving up and down on top of him with her small breasts undulating gently was one of the loveliest things he had ever seen. And then she would make a noise something like a kitten mewing and gasp for breath and fall on top of him while he kissed her small, rosy mouth.

'Was that nice, Sandra?' he would murmur into her hair. Even a girl as vulnerable, as unfinished as her made him feel a need for her approval. Especially in bed.

'It was lovely. You're lovely. You're so beautiful…' she would gush and he would kiss her again to silence her foolishness.

He set her free the way he would have set a little bird free, hoping it would survive. Later, he heard she had become a heroin addict but fortunately her family had the money to send her to rehab for a lengthy treatment. She eventually became a speech therapist, married young – married a doctor with brown hair like his – and had a brood of kids.

Leonora's eldest daughter told Tom Perry, 'My mother was so fat. She had never been so fat. She was thin when they divorced. I was worried with all the anger and stress she would have a stroke.'

Food and clothes were something she could spend money on but they weren't love, they weren't even sex. One well-meaning friend once told Leonora she should find another man. 'Lose some weight. You're still a good-looking woman,' she said. 'You can find someone else.'

Leonora looked at her as if she was mad and left her house without a word. She never spoke to her again. She didn't lose weight and she didn't find another man just then. That was later.

One night, she dreamed she was taking the children to school. It was just a normal day. They were piling in to the car with their schoolbags and she was hurrying them along. All four of them were eventually in the car, bickering and driving her crazy as they did every morning but when she woke and realised it wasn't real, she broke down and sobbed. Such a normal, ordinary thing and how she longed to have it back again. To be their mother again, to be married again, to be Sam's wife again. Normal moments like that were gone and she would never have them again. Now being with her children was like eating some delicious food that someone had put ground glass in. The saying is, You don't know what you've got until it's gone. So very true. Her daughters, in particular, were now so combative, so offensive, so hostile that she could hardly stand to be with them. It tore her heart to pieces to be told by them that she had let them down, that she was crazy or that their father was a better parent. It hurt her so much she said things she didn't mean and didn't want to say and they responded in the same way. It was horrible and she knew it would take years if ever for their relationship to mend. The boys were much more even-handed in how they related to her and to Sam but they were still children. She couldn't bear to think that in time she would have the same kind of hostile conversations with her sons that she had with her daughters.

If she had taken her friend's advice, her obsessive pursuit of Sam might have been curbed or made irrelevant. If she had sought professional help (a new man might have insisted on it) for her grief and rage, she would almost certainly not have killed Sam and Susan. The tragedy is that she became a dangerous, deluded woman and was incapable of listening to good advice or taking it. In the early days of the break-up she feared that seeking psychiatric help or counselling would be used against her to help Sam get full custody but even when that had already happened, she did nothing to help herself. Later, she had given herself over to a rage so incandescent and a hurt so primal that she couldn't stop even if she had wanted to. And she didn't. Rage was her lover and she chose it instead of a man. When Sam moved out, she had bought herself a very expensive fur coat, a $40,000 coat, even though it was the middle of summer. This irrational behaviour only worsened when the divorce became toxic.

But perhaps counselling would never have worked in any case. Early in 1987, Leonora was forced to go to some counselling sessions with a Family Court appointed psychologist. The psychologist, Muriel Portman, found her completely uncooperative, 'unyielding' was the word she used. The sessions were an attempt to resolve the custody battle.

Leonora stated baldly, 'I'm not going to be a single mother with four kids. He'll die first.'

Ominous words. And something else Leonora said concerned Portman deeply.

'The little fuckhead is mine and he'll stay mine.'

Any suggestion that he was no longer hers was met with scorn. Portman even testified that she violated the code of confidentiality because she took Leonora's threats so seriously. She believed Sam was in danger, so she warned him. As it turned out, she was right to do so. All this was going on around the time that Sam began taping Leonora's calls to the children because some of the things they told him involved her making violent threats against him.

It was also around this time that Sam started a wild affair with another doctor, Philomena Graham, a tall, slim, thirty-something redhead with movie star looks and no encumbrances, like a husband for example. She came like a train and was completely insatiable.

'Oh, darling,' she would wail breathlessly as he screwed her senseless. 'My darling, my darling.' She had flawless pale skin.

Sometimes they did it in the pan room at the hospital. The danger made them both gaga. It went on for quite a while.

Portman found it impossible to make Leonora face reality. She simply refused to discuss custody or any of the issues around it.

'I don't want to be a single mother and you can't make me be one,' she told the psychologist, who was thinking at that point that Leonora was like a ship in distress firing on anyone who tried to stop the ship sinking.

Leonora despised single mothers and saw them as immoral failures. She was not an immoral failure and nothing would make her see reason. She had begun keeping a diary three years before and Portman would have been even more concerned if she had read it. The entries were bitter, hysterical and sometimes just mad. In one entry, she claimed that if she killed Sam it was defensible, a form of self-defence. She would be like someone who had killed someone who attacked her family. Sam was responsible for all her suffering and she wanted justice. What form that justice would take was ironically summed up by Sam himself when he told a friend, 'This thing won't end until one of us is dead.' He said it a year before he was killed.

There seemed to be no limits on either side in what had become a war. When Sam proposed to Susan, her daughter Cecilia told Leonora. Her response was to go to Sam's house and take the list of wedding guests which helpfully had their phone numbers next to their names. Susan was efficient and Leonora was on a rampage. She phoned many of the people on the list and threatened that bad things would happen if they went to the wedding. They told Sam, who immediately hired security guards for the wedding. He still regarded Leonora as a figure of fun but now she was becoming a pest too. Susan then went to Leonora's house and persuaded the housekeeper to let her in. She retrieved the list of wedding guests but she also found Leonora's diary. She phoned her and quoted choice passages to her, laughing as she did. Leonora told her friends she felt 'violated'. She got a revolver out of her underwear drawer. Then she went back to Sam's house and retrieved her diary from Susan at gunpoint. Susan told Sam, Sam called the police, but when they went to see Leonora, she denied everything. Said Susan had made it up out of spite.

'That bitch would say anything to get at me,' she snarled. 'I don't even have a bloody gun.'

That was a lie. The gun was Sam's and she had stolen it shortly before he left in the red sports car. It was safely hidden. But Susan had stolen something from her too, that being her husband, and she was going to marry him, the deranged bitch. Susan claimed Leonora was the deranged bitch. There was no proof it had ever happened, no witnesses. Susan's word against hers. The police knew a no-win situation when they saw it. No charges were laid. But having Susan at her mercy at gunpoint was a fine and powerful feeling. She couldn't forget how good it felt.

Cold Heart

Her life was now in free fall. Everything she had worked for and planned for for years now belonged to someone else. Susan had taken her husband and with him everything that made life meaningful and purposeful for Leonora. All of her adult life had been about Sam and their children. She had been the beautiful, gorgeously dressed wife of a handsome, successful and ambitious doctor one minute and in no time at all she was a wife with no husband and a mother with no children. It may have been the law but it was just plain nuts to her. She responded by being nuts herself and that was perhaps not surprising, even if it was not wise. Leonora lacked the skills or the mindset to win against a man using laws written by men for men.

Sam used his brilliant mind to torment Leonora while she stumbled, hurt and bewildered, from one blunder to the next. It was simply impossible for her to believe the man who had shared her bed and fathered her children would never speak to her again. Sometimes, in depression, she thought he was like a predator playing with his prey. Defeating Leonora was so easy it should have been beneath his dignity to torment her as he did but it often seemed to her that the more helpless she was, the more he wanted to annihilate her. Her main complaint against Sam was his coldness. She had truly loved him and given him four children. How could all of that come to nothing and end in hate?

She never grasped that when some men no longer find a woman attractive, even if she happens to be their wife, they feel absolutely entitled to find a woman they do find attractive. Sam was just one of those men. If a woman didn't turn him on ,she was surplus to requirements. It was as if the years they had been together had never happened. They were cancelled out because she didn't go on looking the way she did on their wedding day. To Sam, it was only sensible to be pragmatic, face reality and move on. But Leonora was not able to stop loving Sam, no matter how much she also hated him.

Eventually, she was so depressed and anxious that she often spent hours getting dressed up to go out but then simply could not go. There she sat, dressed up like a fairy princess, staring into space and unable to put one foot in front of the other to leave her house. It was during this era that she ran into Clare's sometime boyfriend, Justin, during one of her early morning walks on the beach.

He later testified that all she talked about was Sam and his treatment of her. 'She called him a piece of shit and said she could kill him for tearing the family apart,' he told the court. He said she made other threats on other occasions but he didn't believe she would ever follow through.

She didn't have any real friends any more. Her constant refrain about Sam and what he had done to her and her bitterness and foul language gradually drove them all away. But did any of them really understand what it was like to lie alone night after night with all your sexual needs unmet? The pain of never being (another word she had come to late in life) fucked, made her skin itch and her clitoris ache. Most agonising of all, she loved a man who now shared his bed with a beautiful younger woman (and, unknown to her, any other beautiful woman he could get his hands on) – a woman who joined him in mocking and goading her. It wasn't just that Leonora no longer felt like a woman. Some days, she actually felt dead. Some days she told herself, 'If I feel this cold, this lonely, this rejected, this isolated, surely I must be dead. I can't still be living, can I?' And that dead feeling only went when she could hate both of them, but Sam most of all, because he was her first and only lover and she still loved him, no matter how much she swore at him and called him names.

It was such torment that the only thing that could describe it was 'the tortures of the damned'. And why was she dammed? What was her sin? All of their married life all she had ever done was love him and their children and what had that got her? That monster, Susan Ross, had her husband now and in the innermost secret depths of her heart she knew she had lost him forever.

Leonora did not know about Sam's serial infidelity. She thought Susan had stolen her husband's love and lured him into infidelity. But thhat was never true. His infidelities had begun when they were not even married and continued up until she shot him. Leonora would tolerate being insulted and even beaten, but not infidelity – and Sam always knew it.

The pain of this illusion, which she could never see for what it was, drove her from crazy act to crazy act, while Sam watched her with disgust and contempt and planned his next move – as if she was a piece on a chessboard. Not a queen. Just a pawn.

Later, she would try to describe her state of mind to the court as she drove with the gun to Sam's house. 'I felt as if I had died and gone to hell, actually. I didn't feel alive,' she said.

Sam got what he wanted. Leonora was temporarily confined to a ward in a psychiatric hospital.

'Once they start playing with guns, there has to be an intervention,' Sam told a psychiatrist, and Leonora was persuaded by Clare and Cecilia to go and see him. The psychiatrist was then able to persuade Leonora that she needed treatment; that it was for her own protection. She certainly knew she was out of control, her rampage was proof if any was needed, so she agreed.

A Day in the Country

While Leonora was in the psych ward, presumably sedated, meaning neutralised for the time being, Sam took a trip to the country with a woman. She had an old-fashioned name, Maureen, but she was not an old-fashioned girl. She was twenty, auburn-haired, tall and slender. An artist. She was very beautiful, of course, or he never would have bothered with her. Ugly women depressed him. She looked like a painting of a Renaissance madonna but she was no madonna. She was always randy. Always touching him and kissing him.

One of the first things she said to him was, 'I love your body.' And she certainly did. She loved kissing his body and sucking his balls. Her skin was as white as milk and her eyes were as blue as the feathers on a blue wren.

It was the weekend and Susan had gone to visit her parents who had retired to the Gold Coast in Queensland. Sam's mother, Glenys, was coming over to stay with the children. She thought Sam was playing golf. That left him gloriously free to take Maureen on a trip to the country. They were going to the Blue Mountains for a picnic.

He pulled out the old picnic basket he'd had for years, which had hardly been used and lived in the storage cupboard under the stairs. Early that morning, he had been to the bakery to buy long, crisp loaves of French bread and other supplies including takeaway chicken, champagne and grapes – and some cherries and peaches for the colour they added to the feast. As an artist, he thought she would appreciate a still life. The only thing he cared about eating was her sweet pussy. He rolled two champagne flutes up in a couple of clean tea towels and carefully packed them in the hamper. Then he spread Mersey Vale cheese over each slice of bread and topped it with chicken before putting another slice of French bread on top. He wrapped the sandwiches in cling wrap and packed them too before adding some serviettes. The fruit he packed on top, and put another tea towel over all of it. Satisfied, he closed the lid of the hamper and put it in a cool part of the kitchen. His mother wouldn't be there for another hour and the children were still sleeping.

His phone rang. It was Maureen.

'Hi, babe,' she chirped. 'What time are you picking me up?'

'Around ten,' he told her. 'Can't wait, can you?' he teased.

'I want you,' she laughed. 'I want you so bad.'

He felt a fluttering in his crotch. 'Don't worry, you'll get me,' he purred, coolly. 'I'm going to push it in as far as it'll go.'

She gave a little shriek of pleasure. The last thing he needed was complications. He didn't want her to get attached.

'See you at ten,' she giggled.

'Yes, at ten. Are you naked?' he whispered.

She gave another even louder shriek and hung up. He decided to take a shower. He smelled like chicken and cheese.

Leonora, meanwhile, was sitting up in bed in her private hospital room, having been judged (mistakenly) to be no danger to herself or others. The sedation had given her the first really good night's sleep she had had for years. But she dreamed all night. Some dreams were nice, others were ghastly, like horror movies, only she was in them. In one of them, she was walking across a suspension bridge over a sheer drop to rocks far below. The bridge broke when she got to the middle and she plunged down in slow motion to the rocks, screaming like an animal. Now, she had to go and see a doctor in the hospital to be assessed for release. She still felt quite mad but she didn't want to stay in this place, so she would have to put on a good act. She got her cosmetic purse and carefully applied make-up and brushed her hair.

Sam and Maureen drove to the Blue Mountains giddy with lust and the clear, sunny spring day. The feeling of sap rising was all-pervading and her hand was on his thigh, not quite touching his penis. He drove in a distracted state but managed to stay on the road and not to speed. She smelled delicious, like spicy vanilla, and she was wearing a pale pink, floral dress that only reached to the middle of her tanned thighs and gold sandals on her tanned feet. Her toenails were painted pink and she was wearing funny little round sunglasses that made her look like a rock star.

'You're beautiful,' he told her.

Her hand moved higher and she dragged her fingers across his penis.

He got hard. 'Stop it! Do you want me to crash the car? 'he mock-scolded.

She giggled and licked his neck. Hot little bitch. He couldn't wait to fuck her in some secluded, hidden place in the shrubbery in the Blue Mountains.

'I hope you want sex,' he teased, 'because that's what you're going to get.'

'My pussy's pulsating,' she sighed and ran her fingers across his penis again.

He started to think he would be walking like Herman Munster by the time he got out of the car, if he could walk at all.

Leonora, made-up and feeling as if it was showtime, was talking to Dr Sanders, the psychiatrist at the hospital. 'I feel so much better,' she was saying. 'I had a really good sleep last night.' No mention of the nightmares which he would have recognised as classic anxiety dreams.

'I can give you a prescription for Valium and as long as you stick to the dose, you can take them temporarily. Until you feel more in control of yourself,' said Dr Sanders.

'Oh, that would be great,' she said plastering a bright, shiny smile on her face. She was a much better actress than she had ever realised.

Dr Sanders smiled too and began writing on his prescription pad. 'Divorce takes its toll. It's a very stressful thing to go through,' he said sympathetically.

Leonora looked at the abstract paintings on his wall and felt completely out of things. As if she was not real and the paintings were. This was better than the feeling she sometimes got that everything was unreal, her and everything around her. But only slightly better.

Sam was on top of Maureen thrusting as if his life depended on it and she was moaning with pleasure with her hand caressing the back of his neck.

'Oh, baby, baby, baby,' she was chanting, as if it was a sacred text. 'Push, push, push. Harder, harder, harder.'

He put his mouth over hers to shut her up and pushed her legs further apart and up so he could get better access to her clitoris. That made her crazy and she began to push back, lifting her arse and him off the ground. She was incredibly strong. That's when a shadow fell across them and Sam looked up to see a man with a rifle.

'What do you think you're doing?' he demanded. 'This is private property.'

Wobbly-legged, Sam got to his feet, zipping his fly. 'Sorry, so sorry,' he babbled.

The man looked at Maureen lying fully exposed in front of him and his mouth got soft and lascivious. She quickly covered up and got to her feet too. Sam thought she looked incredibly beautiful with the sunlight behind her, lighting up her hair.

'We'll go,' she gabbled, out of breath. 'We had no idea it was private property.'

Sam reached into his wallet and pulled out a bundle of notes. 'Take this for any inconvenience,' he told the man, who looked like some kind of crazy survivalist, wearing shorts and a funny looking hat.

The man took the money without a word and without lowering the gun. As they walked away, Sam had no idea if the man would shoot them or not. His back itched, expecting a bullet at any moment. He only felt safe when they got in the car and drove off, wheels spinning and got back on the bitumen road. They laughed hysterically with relief as they drove. The picnic hamper was still in the boot untouched but further up the road they found a picnic area and stopped to have something to eat and drink. They needed it after their near-death experience.

'Crazy bastard!' Sam said. 'Did you see his hat?'

Maureen laughed like mad. 'He looked like he belonged in Kentucky,' she said. 'What a hillbilly freak.'

Years later, Maureen saw the man again. His name was Joe Leske and he was the unwilling star of a documentary detailing the women he had killed. His speciality was attacking courting couples. Wounding the man and raping and killing the woman.

'Fuck,' she shouted to the empty room. 'Fuck, fuck, fuck.' She felt sick and rushed to the fridge to swallow some wine.

But way back when, up in the Blue Mountains, they ended up in a motel where they fucked for three hours and even Maureen was satisfied.

In the car, he put the radio on and Nobody does it Better started playing.

Maureen collapsed in gales of laughter. 'But it's true,' she told him, kissing his hand. 'No one does.'

Sadly, he knew he had to see less of her. She was falling in love with him.

Leonora left the psychiatric hospital with her Louis Vuitton suitcase in one hand and a handbag full of sample prescription drugs given to her gratis by Dr Sanders in the other – and also a prescription for more. How could it be temporary when it seemed so permanent? She was dazed and knew for the first time the meaning of 'a rabbit in the headlights'. She was the rabbit and Sam was the driver. She had to straighten up and fly right or she was going to crash and burn. A mixed metaphor? She wasn't sure. She wasn't sure of anything. She had shadows under her eyes that she had covered with make-up and nothing seemed real, especially not her.

As she walked down the street ,a little girl looked at her and said to her mother, 'That lady looks sick.'

Leonora was furious. As if she needed to be told that she wasn't looking her best. She knew it only too well. The mirror in the bathroom at the hospital was lit by a 100-watt bulb that made her look ancient and completely mad.

She hurried on, anxious to get home as fast as possible. She hailed a cab. Once home, she tipped the drug samples out on to the bed and had a good look at them. There were antidepressants and tranquillisers.

'The antidepressants will help you sleep, the tranquillisers will help you get through the day,' said Dr Sanders.

Was it unkind to call him Dr Feelgood? Leonora smiled cynically. Probably not.

After her trip to the psychiatric hospital, she was rarely unmedicated. A fact that neither side in her court case wanted to bring up, but one that explained, at least to some extent, why she had shot two people in cold blood. The flipside of depression is anger and sometimes that anger is unleashed by antidepressants, as are suicidal thoughts, in some people.

As it turned out, salvation for Leonora came from quite another quarter that had nothing to do with her medical history.

Nemesis

Leonora had always suspected that someone like Susan Ross would appear. In a way, she believed that she had somehow made Susan manifest, that she had conjured her up. Her fear that Sam would not love her and would leave her, made flesh. And what beautiful flesh it was. The first time she saw her she knew, and even though Sam denied it, she still knew. Susan was different. She had that incredible self-assurance. No man was ever going to walk all over her. Susan knew it and any man who was with her knew it. She didn't even have to try: it just came naturally to her. Leonora had been at school with girls like Susan. Top of the class, in the debating team and always looking like the cover of some teenage magazine. In spite of her looks and her relative wealth, Leonora was not like those girls but that was who Susan Ross was. Her beauty, her intelligence, her poise, her cunning decision not to become a lawyer or a doctor or something threatening like that but simply to make men her job, even her profession, was bound to pay off in the end.

Not long after Leonora had begun to suspect the worst, she ran into Susan in a shopping mall. Leonora had just bought a dress, a floral print with a nipped-in waist and off-the-shoulder sleeves. It was black with big white roses all over it. A pretty and flattering dress she planned to wear to a charity garden party she had organised for that day.

'Oh, hello!' said Susan. 'Shopping, I see.'

It sounded like an accusation. Out wasting Sam's money again.

'Oh, yes. It's for a charity event,' Leonora said, pleasantly, but all too eagerly.

'I can't wear dresses like that,' Susan said waspishly, standing there flaunting her impossibly beautiful figure – her tiny waist and hips. 'Dresses like that always make me look hippy,' she giggled.

Leonora's lips actually formed the word 'bitch' but she didn't say it. What Susan was saying was that the dress would make Leonora look hippy. It all confirmed in Leonora's mind that Susan was indeed fucking her husband and would no more give him up than a lioness would loosen her grip on a wildebeest. She felt sick to her stomach. She actually thought she might vomit but she took a breath and swallowed hard and the feeling went away.

'I admire you so much for all that charity work you do,' smarmed Susan. 'I can't of course. I have to work,' she said with a smirk, tossing her hair back as if she was at a photoshoot. The subtext being 'Get off your arse and get a job you lazy stay at home mum.'

Just breathe, Leonora told herself. Just breathe. 'Of course. But the charity events I organise are work too, believe me. They don't just run themselves,' she said with a bright, false smile on her face.

'I'm sure they don't. It must be hard getting all those rich people to part with their money,' Susan said. Snipe. Snipe. Rich people like you, Leonora. They have to be entertained and have their egos stroked before they will do the right thing.

'It might be cheaper just to go door to door with a bucket,' Susan laughed, her eyes glittering with hate and contempt. 'But then you wouldn't get to wear that nice dress, would you?' she added, her beautiful head on the side as she searched for something in her handbag. 'Those damn car keys,' she purred. 'I need a man to – er – organise me,' and she laughed prettily and fished the keys out of her handbag. 'Found them. Well, I have to go. I have to buy some pork chops and apple sauce. See ya.' She waved her fingers at Leonora and walked off down the street as if she was on a catwalk.

Leonora stood there furious and humiliated. Pork chops and apple sauce was Sam's favourite meal. She knew who Susan was cooking for. She had never known that she could hate someone the way she hated Susan Ross. It made her weak in the knees to hate like that. She wasn't used to it and it made her afraid.

The charity garden party began at two in the afternoon and was held in the grounds of the mansion of another member of the Committee for Finding a Cure for Cancer. Muriel Eckhardt's husband was a developer and Muriel Eckhardt looked like Brigitte Bardot's daughter if she had had one. She was a knockout and it had paid off handsomely for her. A good-looking husband, richer than God, and four stunning teenage daughters with the same blue eyes, blonde hair and Barbie Doll body she had. The mansion had ocean views and a garden that was worked on by three gardeners on a daily basis. A large white marquee tent stood in between two enormous trees with the sparkling ocean as a backdrop. Champagne flowed and glasses clinked. There was even a fountain gurgling away.

Leonora arrived in her pretty off-the-shoulder dress and Muriel air kissed her and handed her a glass of champagne.

'Know your speech?' she teased.

'I'll manage,' Leonora laughed. 'A bit more champagne and I'll be fine.'

And then she saw her. Susan Ross was standing under one of those huge trees wearing white. A sleeveless white dress of linen with a chic black collar and three strands of pearls at her throat. They looked real and Leonora realised, as if she was in bad dream, that Sam must have given them to her. Susan looked ravishing with her hair pulled up into a chignon. She was a beauty and she knew it, so she was posing, leaning up against the tree.

Muriel noticed that Leonora was staring at Susan (she hardly even knew she was, it all seemed so unreal) and she took her arm.

'Come and meet the newest member of the committee,' Leonora heard Muriel saying, and before she could make an excuse she was walking her over to meet Susan.

Leonora's face felt frozen. She couldn't smile. 'I know Susan,' she managed to get out and Muriel, to her horror, said, 'I'll leave you two to chat,' and disappeared.

Face to face with her nemesis, she had no choice but to make nice. 'I didn't know you were coming,' Leonora said. 'You didn't say.'

Susan gave her a contemptuous smirk and turned her back and walked away.

'You bitch,' Leonora said loud enough for her to hear as she watched her retreating back and her tiny hips in that white dress. 'I know you're fucking my husband.'

Susan stopped walking, turned around and laughed at her. 'He told me you thought that,' she said and just kept walking.

What did that mean? Was she denying it? Trying to make her think she was crazy? Her head was swimming. She felt as if she would faint and she still had to give that speech. No more champagne. She knew how much Susan Ross would love to see her fall on her face, fall from the dais while she was giving the speech.

As it turned out, she gave the speech without a hitch but not without feeling panic clutching at her. When she looked into the crowd gathered to hear the speech, she could see Susan – like a white beacon – staring up at her with hate and *Schadenfreude*, but she pretended to herself that Susan wasn't there. That she didn't exist. If only it was true.

Leonora made an early escape from the garden party and when she got home Sam was sprawled on the couch watching football.

'That bitch was at the garden party. Did you know she was going?'

'What are you talking about? What garden party?' he said, looking bored.

But of course he didn't know. He took absolutely no interest in anything she did any more.

'The cancer charity I'm on the committee of. Susan Ross was there making a nuisance of herself. Mocking me and trying to pretend she isn't fucking you.'

'Don't talk that way, the children will hear you!' he said furiously.

'Oh, of course. I can't say it but you can do it. You hypocrite.'

He got up off the couch, took her by the arms and shook her. 'Shut up! You lunatic!' he screamed at her.

She smacked his face and he punched her and laid her out unconscious on the floor. Ever the caring father, he shut the door so the children wouldn't see, carried her into the bedroom and threw her on the bed. The off-the-shoulder dress now had blood on it. He shut the bedroom door and went back to the football as if nothing had happened.

Clare opened the door and put her head around the door frame. 'Where's Mum?'

'She's having a lie down. She came home tired,' he lied. 'You know how she is with all these charity things.'

'I wanted to ask her about…'

'No,' Sam said in his I-mean-business voice. 'Don't disturb her.'

Clare went back to her room.

Thank God, Sam thought, she hadn't seen what her mother had made him do. Leonora just asked for it sometimes. What good was talking about Susan to him going to do? What did she want him to say? He had lied to her about Susan from the start and he wasn't going to start telling the truth now.

Stripped and Jailed

After she was arrested, she spent her first night in custody in the police cells. She was in a state of shock.

'I was completely naked, I slept naked. I was distraught. I was on suicide watch. I just did as I was told,' she later told the court.

She was now moving to phase three of her life. Phase one – golden girl. Phase two – abandoned wife. Phase three – murderous loony. The story was all over the papers and all over the TV news. There were also magazine articles complete with photos of Leonora, Sam and their children – and of course there were photos of Susan looking gorgeous. Thankfully, there were none of her dead body tangled in bloody sheets. This wasn't a murder in Western Sydney. Working-class people drunkenly killing each other. This was high society and everyone involved looked good in photos and had perfect teeth. Manna from heaven for the media.

Sam's friends lined up to tell Tom Perry that Sam was the innocent victim of a crazed woman who just couldn't let go. Men who kill unfaithful wives often claim temporary insanity, diminished responsibility and sometimes get lighter sentences as a result. A violent response to being betrayed or discarded could be seen by some people as a normal response in a man. Tom Perry thought O.J. Simpson depended on that as much as the bloody glove to get acquitted of a murder he obviously committed.

Leonora was denied bail and corrective services took her to Silverwater, a tough prison for a tough woman, most people would have thought. But despite appearances, Leonora was not tough. She was terrified.

Praise for Sam poured in. Many newspaper articles featured commentary from work colleagues, fellow doctors, describing Sam as a 'wonderful doctor with a brilliant mind' with a 'gift for diagnosis' and a 'father who despite his heavy workload, made time for his kids'. His long torture and degradation of Leonora never rated a mention. His legal manoeuvring to strip her of everything and get her locked up in psych ward was also missing in action. Another staple of these stories was the fact that Sam had armed guards at his wedding to Susan. They called Leonora a 'socialite', which upped the glamour factor but was not strictly true. The image these stories created of Leonora was of a re-venge-crazed airhead and a greedy, gold-digging bitch. They also often presented a triggering event for Leonora's outburst of homicidal vio-lence: Sam and Susan were planning to start a family.

'Leonora was crazy with jealousy and rage,' one of her 'friends' told Tom Perry. 'No one was ever going to have babies with Sam except Leonora, even though she couldn't any more because she had a tubal ligation.'

The newly-weds were also thinking of moving to Melbourne. In fact, the triggering factor had nothing to do with either of those things.

Sam and Susan's funeral took place on 3 December while Leonora sat in Silverwater awaiting trial. A friend who was allowed to attend (Leonora was not, even if they would have let her out of jail for it) told her they had matching coffins of white. Sam's was covered in red roses while Susan's was covered in white roses. Current affairs shows covered every aspect of the case, carefully, because under *sub judice* rules they couldn't say anything deemed prejudicial to the case. It was in between Leonora's first trial and the second that the media was let off the leash a bit, just enough to make it almost impossible for her to get a fair trial. They painted her as a half-crazed witch lusting for blood.

When Clare visited her mother in jail, Leonora at first showed no re-morse and tried to persuade her shocked daughter that she had had no choice but to kill Sam. She couldn't, she explained, let him go on living with that whore and corrupting the morals of their children. She also told Clare she had no choice but to be on her side and that she would be out soon and they would go shopping. Clare was actually scared of her mother at this point, she told Tom Perry, afraid as she put it of the 'madness in her eyes'. She was interviewed by Tom Perry before Leonora's second trial began, and she said her mother screamed at her, calling her a 'traitor' when she argued with her mother's justification for the murder of her father.

'You've always been daddy's girl!' she had shouted at her terrified daughter. 'Well, just see how far worshipping men will get you, you fool.'

'You're the one who goes in for that! Look at how you say he treated you and you stayed with him,' Clare shouted back. 'You even claim he beat you. If that's true, why didn't you leave?'

Leonora dissolved in tears, head in her hands, crying like a child.

'She's like that,' Clare told Tom Perry. 'A ferocious bitch one minute and a sobbing little girl the next. I love her but I don't always like her,' she added.

Tom Perry thought he wouldn't like to get on the wrong side of either of them.

Leonora's lawyer, Darren Rabinowitz, speaking to Tom Perry before her second trial, said he doubted Leonora's side of things would come out. Sam, he said, had used the legal profession to take everything from his ex-wife, until she felt like a cornered animal. Her side of the story would not be told by the media. His was one of the very few voices raised in her defence. Rabinowitz claimed her case was no different to one of 'battered wife syndrome'; it was just that the weapon Sam used to beat his wife was the legal system. He was only vaguely aware of Sam's actual beatings of his wife and even if he had been aware, there was no evidence they had ever taken place because Leonora never reported them to the police. Rabinowitz also stated that the majority of Sam's assets had been 'hidden', moved into his friend Kevin's businesses so that

Leonora could never share them. He left her with scraps while Susan and he sat at a table enjoying a banquet. His behaviour was despicable and meant to provoke Leonora into a mental collapse so that he could have her confined to a psychiatric hospital.

People had been talking incessantly since Leonora's arrest and nothing they said was helpful to her case.

When questioned, Clare told the police her mother admitted that she had shot Sam: about two days after she shot him, she had 'remembered'.

Ellen Brown described to police how Leonora told her that she thought she had fired a gun but couldn't really remember.

Another ex-friend confirmed that Leonora told her she shot Sam but that she didn't know if he was dead because the room was so dark. She didn't mention Susan; it was as if she was collateral damage to Leonora. She expressed no remorse over either death.

She told Tom Perry, 'They talk about how they are victims. The fact is they wanted to destroy me and both of them destroyed my family. They were selfish morons.'

Leonora would have made an excellent general and scorched earth would have been her favourite strategy.

Leonora made a friend in jail: Kay Tait. She was also a murderess; she had stabbed her lover twenty times. They were both held in a unit separate from the other prisoners. Fortunately they got on famously. Leonora told the court during her trial that she was happy to be locked up. She said she felt safe where 'no one can harm me'. Irony was never her strong point. Leonora could only see one victim in the whole saga, and that was her. Like most girls, she was brought up to believe that if a girl was good (meaning chaste) and was loving and faithful to her husband, she would be cherished and he would be faithful in return. The truth hit her like a sledgehammer – it ain't necessarily so. This turned her entire belief system on its head and the feelings of rage brought on by it drove her to go on pursuing Sam when he was already in love with Susan and also had his many amours to satisfy him and didn't want her any more. To her, the injustice and inhumanity with which she had been treated by both Susan and Sam was a deal breaker. 'It wasn't supposed to be like this,' was the thought that kept running round and round her head. She didn't know how to make it stop and sometimes she wanted to scream at the top of her voice, 'I didn't do anything to deserve this. I kept my half of the bargain.'

But Sam wouldn't even speak to her.

The nastiness was everywhere at that time and left no one in Leonora's immediate family untouched.

Leonora told Tom Perry that Sam had even phoned Leonora's mother, Antonella, and ordered her to call Leonora off as if she was an out of control attack dog. Leonora's father then came on the phone and called Sam 'a lying, depraved cunt'. Sam hung up.

Clare later told Tom Perry that Leonora flew into a rage when she found out she had turned to Susan for help when she needed an abortion. In retaliation, Clare told the journalist that Leonora, the devoted Catholic, had also had an abortion. All the family secrets came spilling out: untidy and inconvenient.

Sam's friend, Kevin, in his conversation with Tom Perry, called the shootings 'executions'.

Even Leonora's diary was now a legal document – evidence. Her life and her marriage, not to mention her character, could now possibly be dissected in a death of a thousand cuts by the media.

Jury selection began while the defence and the prosecution squabbled over how much anything in the diary was relevant to the shootings.

Crim/ology

It's what everyone wants to know. Why did she do it? After all, many women have been treated as badly as she was. They did not kill their husbands. Maybe they ended up on tranquillisers or antidepressants – or both when one or the other didn't work – and maybe they just divorced, moved away, went back to school, met another man or did any number of things that Leonora did not do or only did late in the piece after she had killed Sam. What made her different?

Rabinowitz sat brooding on his deck as the sun went down and his wife bustled around in the kitchen preparing an evening meal for their family of five. Orange, reds and golds streaked the sky in a fiery display and the trees were dark shapes against the sky.

Attempts to explain what is called 'the criminal mind' have gone on for centuries. Sue Titus Reed refers to it in *Crime and Criminology*, a book Rabinowtiz read as an undergraduate. Psychopaths and neurotics, obsessives, sadists, masochists, pyromaniacs, sexual predators – the list is extensive. Some psychologists tried to explain the criminal mind in terms of intelligence, or lack of it. How people came to commit crimes was not explored while low intelligence or lack of impulse control was put forward as an explanation. In the twentieth century, social scientists began to research the factors that led one person to become a criminal while others did not. Demonic possession was one of the oldest explanations and the person suffering from it was usually banished. In the medieval era, it was priests who were charged with getting rid of the demon that had possessed someone. Flogging was sometimes used to drive out the demon. In the fifteenth century, it was decided that the person who had become possessed was working with the devil and was choosing to do so. This led to witch hunts and the burning of witches at the stake. In the eighteenth century, knowledge was gathered on anatomy, physiology, neurology, medicine and chemistry. This led to demonology being replaced by a medical approach based on the idea that psychological problems could cause mental illness and also cause people to commit crimes like murder.

Sigmund Freud, as Rabinowitz had read in Titus Reed's book, maintained that we all have criminal impulses but, due to proper socialisation as children, the tendencies are curbed. Curbed, but not destroyed. Not eradicated. Those impulses remain but will be controlled unless some kind of mental imbalance sets in, such as extreme jealousy, sexual obsession, uncontrollable possessiveness, some insult to a person's self-esteem from which they cannot recover. Then the person can revert to a semi-infantile state where all the assertive and aggressive traits, which Freud saw as the norm in human beings – an inborn tendency to violence which is repressed under normal circumstances to fit in with society's mores – reappear. Freud saw these tendencies as being repressed and stored in the subconscious: but when a person becomes mentally unbalanced, then these tendencies can be acted out. They leave the subconscious and become part of the conscious mind and cause people to commit crimes that many of their friends and relatives can scarcely believe them capable of. The truth, according to Freud, is that we all have what are seen as criminal and deviant tendencies but most of us never act on them.

Rabinowitz could remember some passionate debates from his university days on this subject.

'So we're all just rats in some giant laboratory?' said Danny Dodds, a red-haired oddball, full of eccentric theories on almost everything: but on murder he was a conservative. No murderer had an excuse and no murderer was ever innocent. 'Murderers are stupid. That's the worst thing about them and if they're not punished society will become another version of the Coliseum!' he exclaimed, knocking his coffee over in his enthusiasm.

'And the death penalty?'

'Yes, of course. They need to pay for their crime. An eye for an eye and a tooth for a tooth.'

He later became a judge. It made Rabinowitz snicker to think of his frustration at not having the death penalty to impose.

Leonora was unlucky, according to this Freudian theory of human behaviour. If Sam had not left her and treated her with coldness and cruelty, she would almost certainly never have killed. In *Crime and Criminology*, Sue Titus Reed references studies which have shown that people with high self-esteem are much less likely to commit crimes than those with low self-esteem. If that was true, Sam's tactic of encouraging Leonora to have low self-esteem, both by beating her and being cold and rejecting in everyday life, increased the possibility that she would commit a crime. In his case, that proved lethal. 'Hell hath no fury like a woman scorned' describes someone whose image of themselves has been so damaged that it makes them unhinged – even if only temporarily and even if it doesn't lead to murder. Premenstrual tension is defined as a legal form of insanity in France, according to Titus Reed, and has been used to attain reduced sentences in England.

Rabinowitz mused on all this as his wife brought him a glass of red wine. 'Red wine,' he said to his wife, Lara, who was a pretty, blonde thirty-something and also a lawyer. 'Remember that case in Germany?'

'The one where that woman was acquitted of murdering her lover?'

'Yes. I can still remember reading about it in a German magazine. I was shocked she got off – how things have changed.'

'Have they?'

'Yes. This case has shown me a whole new world of mitigation.'

'Really? You're turning into a feminist, are you?' Lara said laughing.

He wasn't, but he well recalled that case in Germany where a woman was acquitted of murder because she had been drinking red wine waiting for her lover to show and he was hours late. The red wine was held to have sent her into a murderous rage and she killed her lover because of it. Red wine was known to have that effect on some people. Fortunately for her.

Rabinowitz asked Lara, 'Have you ever felt like killing someone? Have you ever been that angry?'

She looked at him, raised her eyebrows and gave it some thought. 'No,' she said. 'There was that girl in high school…' she laughed. 'I would have liked to have a voodoo doll to stick pins in but I would never have killed her. Then there was Dan who gave me a really bad time when I was eighteen but I just dumped him, because I knew he was going to dump me. He was a bit of a psycho, I think, but I didn't want to kill him. I've never actually wanted to kill anyone – not even you.' She kissed the top of his head and pulled a face.

He smacked her backside and kissed her neck.

'Ooooh, naughty,' she cooed.

He suspected he would be having a good time in bed that night. She left to check on the lasagne in the oven and he watched her lovely body as she went. Then he watched an owl flapping around in the trees trying to find a branch to settle on before it began its nocturnal hunt for food. Sometimes, he couldn't help thinking that the owls had the best of it. They killed every night and no one condemned them for it. The red wine made him feel like sleeping but there was all that lasagne to eat first.

Homicide du Jour

The jury selection process is intended to remove from serving on the jury anyone who has already formed an opinion on the accused's guilt or innocence. That left a jury of six women and six men to decide Leonora's fate. In age, they ranged from people in their sixties to twenty-five-year-olds and they were employed in a wide range of professions and occupations. Not quite a jury of Leonora's peers but close enough.

Leonora looked fantastic – she had lost another five kilos in prison. Her hair was blonde and bobbed. She wore a series of stylish suits and looked every inch a lady. The jurors found it hard to believe she had shot two people in cold blood. That was, of course, her and her lawyer's intention. The courtroom was packed – there were queues for seats and a daily, dignified struggle to get a front row seat. Everyone was talking about the case: not just the media but people in gyms, hairdressers and coffee shops. Everyone had an opinion. It was a case that polarised the public. And it was as much a performance as any play in a theatre. But, of course, being unrehearsed, there would be surprises along the way.

The prosecution was conducted by Moira Reynolds, who was more at home in the Family Court. Thirty-five years old, fair-haired and slender, and tallish with intelligent blue eyes, she was completely convinced of Leonora's guilt. She thought it was a horrible murder but worse than that, a senseless murder. She told her husband over dinner one night, 'Why didn't she just take a lover and go back to uni and get another degree? She had so many options, but hate blinded her. She just wanted revenge. Someone took something that she thought was hers – her husband – and that was not to be endured.'

Moira Reynolds had no problem going after Leonora with a kind of implacable precision.

Rabinowitz watched her stride into the courthouse wearing a neat taupe suit under her robe and long brown boots up to her knees and murmured to his junior, Bettina Clark, 'The Valkyrie is here.'

But Reynolds was no zealot – she leaned to the left on most issues, she believed in rehabilitation and was firmly opposed to the death penalty. Fortunately for Leonora, there wasn't one in Australia.

During the trial, Moira Reynolds had witnesses who implied that Leonora never loved Sam – that she only married him because she knew he would eventually be worth a lot of money. Her parents were ambitious aspirationals themselves and expected her to marry a doctor or a lawyer. Antonella's face turned stony during some of this testimony. According to Reynolds, Leonora's rage all stemmed from having lost her affluent and glamorous lifestyle. But none of that really made sense. Leonora was a woman scorned, and possessed by jealousy and anger as a consequence. Her fanatical conviction that Sam was hers and only hers, in spite of all evidence to the contrary, was caused by the sexual jealousy that tortured her day and night. A woman who had married for (ultimate) material gain would not have wanted to be around Sam and would not have suffered as she did when he found another woman, left her and then married that other woman. She was like someone suspended over a pit of flames and those flames weren't burning because of money.

Reynolds in her no-nonsense way explained to the court that Leonora was living in a beautiful home, had $16,000 a month at her disposal and was never going to be poor, never going to go hungry under the financial arrangements that Sam had made for her. But it was never enough. All of that overlooked the humiliation, the loss of self-esteem Sam's affair, the divorce and his subsequent remarriage put her through. To state as Reynolds did that the case was only about revenge and hate was to ignore the labyrinthine complexities of a woman's sexual attachment to a man. And that attachment never ended for Leonora. It would be much truer to say that Leonora never stopped loving Sam and couldn't bear for another woman to have him. But Reynolds was too clever a lawyer to even refer to sexual jealousy as a motive. That would have opened a can of worms covering crimes of passion and diminished responsibility.

To call what Leonora was feeling 'hate' ignored the ferocious sexual jealousy towards the woman who had replaced her which would not have been there had Leonora not still loved Sam. Nor would she have spent so much time behaving like a child in order to get him to speak to her or to give her his attention. As she did by trying to literally burn the house down and ramming her car into the front of the house he shared with Susan. Even the use of the words 'fuck', 'fuckhead' and 'cunt' were a desperate cry for attention but they only disgusted Sam and pushed him further away. He hated it when women used foul language, even though he used it himself. All of that made Leonora irrational, Rabinowitz contended.

The case Reynolds presented was that it was just cold, calculated and premeditated murder but Leonora told Tom Perry she went to the beach first, with the gun, because she planned to kill herself. Perry thought ththatis showed a woman at the end of her rope: but she didn't kill herself. Her story was that she went to Sam's house with the gun because she thought with it in her hand she could force him to listen to her. Either he would listen to her and give her some respect, realise that he still loved her or she would end her suffering once and for all.

'I wanted to shoot myself in front of them. I wanted them to acknowledge my pain,' she told the police after she was arrested. She always claimed she had no intention of shooting Sam and Susan but no one in their right mind could have believed that going to Sam's house with a gun would end well. Therefore, she was not in her right mind at the time of the shootings. That was more or less the defence's case.

One example of Reynolds's claim that Leonora acted in a cold, calculating way was the story that she ripped the phone out to prevent anyone calling the police. That was done, argued Reynolds, in a cool calculating way. She needed time to kill them and didn't want any interruptions or to be thwarted in her plan.

Rabinowitz rebutted the claim by showing a crime scene photo that showed the phone lying where it had been forcefully thrown with the wires dangling on the floor after being ripped out of the wall. That was done by a woman who was completely out of control, he said. Not in the calm, purposeful way the prosecution claimed.

On the other hand, Leonora's own daughter, Clare, testified that shortly before Sam married Susan her mother told her she was going to shoot both of them. She even told her she would shoot them 'in the head, three or four times'. Asked about her mother's demeanour, Clare said she 'looked mad, she was ranting like a madwoman'. She did shoot Susan in the head, once, but she only managed to shoot Sam in the lung, arm and legs not the head – presumably because he was moving around and trying to avoid being shot. He took longer to die, as a consequence.

Clare's testimony was potentially devastating and painted a vivid picture of the dysfunctional relationship between her and her mother. Some jurors looked shocked when Clare testified that her mother told her, 'You make me sick. You make me want to vomit. Why were you ever born?' But other jurors asked themselves how they could believe what Clare said about her mother when they had such a toxic relationship.

Rabinowitz told the court that Leonora had been 'bullied for years and we all know how that ends.' Susan, he claimed, had the power to make Sam behave decently towards Leonora but she did not. Instead she joined in the bullying and humiliation – which was, he said, why she shot both of them.

Most of all what Rabinowitz presented as the trigger that precipitated Leonora's actions were the words Leonora heard one of them say, 'Call the police!' It was what Sam always said when she came to his house and tried to talk to him and it sent her into an uncontrollable rage. She silenced them both. They would never say those words to her again.

Leonora's Testimony

Her only hope of avoiding a first-degree murder conviction was to take the stand and share her suffering and her mistreatment (as she saw it) at the hands of her ex-husband. It was risky but Leonora was in such a bad way emotionally that if even some small measure of her pain reached the jury, it would work in her favour. She had admitted firing the gun. She had repeatedly told people she would kill them both. She had even specified to her daughter, Clare, that she would shoot them three of four times in the head. Her only hope was to throw herself on the mercy of the jurors and convince them that losing Sam and his treatment of her after she had lost him had made her mad and sad enough to kill him and his new wife in a moment of unplanned and uncontrollable rage. She had a lot of damming evidence, she told herself, to present to the jurors.

'When we went for marriage counselling, he told me he was sorry he couldn't be the father and the husband he wanted to be just then; but he wanted to be rich, he wanted to be socially important, he wanted me and the children to have everything, he told me. Soon we would be there, he assured me. I just had to give him more time. All of it would be worth it in the end, but in the end he left me for a twenty-five-year-old and tried to take most of the fruits of my sacrifices away from me. He succeeded too. I only cared what he thought of me. Everything I did was for him. But in 1983, my horror year, he told me I was fat, dumb and dull. He told me I wasn't fun. I was shocked. I loved him and I had built my life around him. And he talks to me like that? I can't even describe the pain I felt.'

A couple of women jurors wiped away tears, causing Moira Reynolds to bite her lips.

Why did she drop the children off one by one at Sam's house?

'I wanted him to understand my contribution to our family. He didn't value me. I wanted him to see I had value,' Leonora told the court, sobbing.

She burned his suits, 'Because they meant more to him than our family. He was so materialistic, so obsessed with how he looked, how other people saw him. That falseness made me sick. Just because a man has an expensive suit and cuts a fine figure in society doesn't make him a good person. He didn't care what I thought of him, only what strangers thought of him.'

She rammed her car into the door of the house Sam and Susan shared, 'Because Sam wouldn't talk to me. He would never talk to me. He would always yell, "Call the police!" if ever I showed up and wanted to talk to him. That made me so angry and frustrated. I needed him to listen and he wouldn't. He lied to me for so long and I believed him. When he was with Susan, he told me he wasn't and I believed him. I felt like a complete fool when he finally admitted he was sleeping with her. It made me feel as if I was having breakdown.' She paused for effect. 'How could he do that?'

On the second day of her testimony, the queues to get into the court were even longer. Word had spread that this was the best show in town.

She told the court that in 1992 she was under attack from all sides. Legal documents were flying at her from all directions. And she wasn't allowed to see her children, 'Because he lied about me constantly. He just couldn't stop lying.'

In 1992, that fateful morning of 3 November , she woke very early. She had breakfast and then she checked the letter box. There was another letter from Sam's lawyers: it told her that she would not be seeing her children for months. Sam was taking them and Susan on an overseas trip and they would be living in France. He thought it would be good for them, culturally.

'I knew I couldn't go on,' she told Tom Perry. 'I couldn't stand it another day. I decided I would be better off dead. That's why I went down to the beach to shoot myself. So of course I had the gun with me when I went to Sam's place. But I wasn't able to shoot myself. I just sat in the sand crying. I decided I should go and see Sam and take the gun with me so I could make him listen to me. I wasn't thinking clearly but I had some vague plan to shoot myself in front of them. I was about to be forty-two, this crap had been going on since I was thirty-five. Seven years. Seven years bad luck. Sam and Susan were telling people I was a child molester, that I was crazy, that I was not able to be a mother to my children. All these thoughts were running around in my head. I wanted to tell Sam that the legal stuff had to stop. It was ruining both our lives, ruining the kids' lives. I took the gun because Sam had been violent to me when we were married. He roughed me up, gave me a black eye, left marks. I never had a broken bone or anything like that but it was more good luck than good management. Sam wanted me in jail or in a psych ward. I just couldn't face being in jail again. Ironic in view of my present situation. If he wouldn't listen, I decided I would shoot myself. Splash my blood all over their bedroom.'

The female jurors' faces if they had heard any of this would have been a study in mixed emotions.

'How many shots did you hear?' Rabinowitz asked Leonora during her testimony.

'I don't remember hearing any. I don't remember firing the gun. I just remember how dark the room was. So dark that later I couldn't believe I had actually hit anyone when they told me they were dead.'

Her cross-examination by Moira Reynolds was an attack. Leonora was grilled over the details of the legal documents she claimed were coming at her from all directions.

Leonora admitted that due to stress there were a lot of things she simply could not remember.

'Didn't you write in your diary around this time that Susan would never have a child because you would kill her first? Didn't you write that she hadn't conceived so far because you had put a curse on her?'

'If you say that is true,' she told Reynolds, 'then it probably is. My life at that time was that I was being eaten alive by stress. There is so much, so many details I simply cannot recall. Sam kept telling me I was crazy – and in the end I was.'

At times, Leonora seemed to want to help Reynolds out. 'You seem confused,' she told her. 'I can help you. THIS is what happened.'

When Reynolds questioned her over perceived inconsistencies in her story, Leonora told her, 'I was gang raped by the legal system for years and I was not myself in the end, so things I've said or say may not be one thousand per cent correct but believe me I have been as accurate as I could be under the circumstances.'

That allowed Reynolds to ask her, 'So you admit some of your "facts" could be inaccurate?'

'Some, but overall most of what I've said is true and factual,' Leonora replied.

All of this won her, not Reynolds, points with the jury.

Reynolds also tried to downplay or discredit her story that Sam had been violent to her during their marriage.

'As I recall,' Leonora told the court, 'it was his elbow that gave me a black eye. It wasn't the only time and at the time it wasn't a big deal. I don't know why, now, but that's how it was then.'

Reynolds then put it to her that the photo that had been in the papers and in some magazine articles of her with a black eye was fake. That, in fact, it was mascara artfully smudged around her eye and that it had been done to win her sympathy during the decisions over who would get custody of the children. Hadn't friends confirmed that it was fake?

'Hah,' snorted Leonora. 'With friends like those, I don't need any enemies, do I?'

The entire courtroom erupted into laughter.

'I took that photo myself. I'm still not sure why. Maybe just to record what he had done. Perhaps I thought I could pull it out one day when he was being a shit and remind him that with all my faults I was not a basher, and he was. I don't know what my plan was. Mainly, I suppose I was in disbelief – I always was when he did things like that – and needed proof. I mean, after all, he was a doctor.'

The word 'doctor' hung in the air like a discordant note, so Reynolds changed tack.

'You spent $50,000 on clothes in 1986, is that correct?'

'I may have spent $50,000 but I deny it was on clothes. That was the year I took the children away for Christmas. Sam gave me nothing extra towards that.'

'You've pleaded not guilty to murder,' Reynolds said, 'but is it not a fact that you shot Susan so that she could not inherit Sam's estate? You knew exactly what you were doing, didn't you?'

'I was a basket case. I was suicidal and not thinking rationally. All I really wanted was for Sam to listen to me and not call the police. If he had done that, it would have all been different. I was on medication but even with the medication I wasn't sleeping.'

Reynolds then moved on to the suicide attempt in 1983. Why had Leonora not called a doctor? Wasn't it just theatre? An attempt to get Sam's attention?

'Sam was a doctor. He assessed my condition and told me I was in no danger. He bandaged my wrists. It was the first time he'd touched me in a long time. If you're asking did I really want to die, the answer is yes, I did. I did it right-handed with a man's razor.' She pointed to her wrists. 'There's a scar. There's another scar. I made a mess of it, clearly, because I didn't die, but there are scars. Naturally, not all of the scars from that little episode are visible.'

Rabinowitz was seen to give a little smile.

In between the first and second trials, Leonora stated in an interview with Tom Perry that Sam and Susan had tortured her, quite deliberately.

'What did they have to gain from not letting me see my children? Constantly robbing me of everything for no reason I could see. She could have been kind, she could have made him behave decently – she had a complete stranglehold over him – but she chose not to and to instead join in the bullying, the insults, the degradation of me as a woman and as a human being.'

During the first trial, Rabinowitz introduced a notebook into evidence which came from the marriage counselling weekend in 1976. In it, Sam stated, 'I know I have to earn lots of money, establish myself as a doctor, acquire desirable possessions before I can indulge in the luxury of being an attentive, considerate husband.'

The jurors looked stunned. Since when, they asked themselves, had being a considerate, attentive husband been a luxury? An indulgence?

This kind of evidence didn't go over well with Sam's family either.

Afterwards, outside the court, on the pavement Sam's brother, Kevin, told the assembled media, 'This woman (Leonora) is a monster. Sam had to live with her endless greed and hate for years. It makes me sick to think of what she put him through.'

There was no mention of what Sam had put her through. No mention of the mountain of evidence that Sam deliberately set out to drive Leonora into a mental breakdown because he wanted full custody of their children. His treatment of her was cruel and, to any uninvolved outsider, also unnecessary.

'He could have behaved well but he chose not to,' Leonora mused to Tom Perry, 'mainly because it didn't advantage him financially or otherwise.'

And ultimately that selfishness and tunnel vision led to the loss of his own life and the death of the woman he claimed to love.

Friends, Doctors and a Lover

The defence left no stone unturned in their effort to show that Leonora had been driven to firing that gun in that dark bedroom because Sam had made her mad, deliberately, to advantage himself in the divorce.

First came a psychologist with many years' experience in divorce cases – and the fallout for women. His other areas of expertise, chillingly, were post shooting trauma and post-traumatic stress disorder.

'When a husband is unfaithful, it is sometimes so traumatic for the wife that she can exhibit some of the symptoms of PTSD. If the man has also lied about the infidelity for a long time, a wife can experience deep shame and humiliation. She asks herself how she could have been so gullible and so foolish. A sense of unreality sets in, such as occurs in very traumatic situations,' Dr Rod Galen told the court. 'She wonders how this can have happened to her. She fears the future and this is compounded when the woman is no longer young. Money becomes a substitute for affection and security she previously enjoyed – if she can't have love, she'll have money – and if she is thwarted in that, a tremendous rage can develop. If the husband and wife can remain on good terms and the wife is treated with respect and fairness, the situation can be defused. But when the opposite occurs, the consequences can be disastrous.'

He suggested that was what had happened with Leonora. 'It seems that Sam Davison put a lot of effort into making his wife mentally unstable, causing her to behave in extreme ways because it strengthened his case for full custody of his children. What he seems never to have considered was that she could be pushed up to and beyond her breaking point. Some people, including people who specialise in counselling those going through divorce, believe she did break under the relentless stress and the contempt and disrespect from both her husband and his new wife.'

Rabinowitz also called a clinical therapist with years of experience on the effects of extramarital affairs. Dr Dennis Brown was a dapper professional man in his fifties with kind blue eyes.

'A woman with an unfaithful husband can become suicidal. She may also threaten her husband,' he told the court. 'It can go either way because she has been deceived by a man she may still love, her life partner, and it hurts. The wound is deep, very deep. Finding out about infidelity throws her entire life with that partner into doubt. Was it all a lie? Did he ever love her? She begins to question everything. If the divorce goes badly, if the husband is hostile and combative, it's another wound. Only the ex-husband can fix it. And he can only fix it by behaving decently and being fair. There's no other cure. No legal remedy. It seems clear to me that Sam Davison did not behave well and was often grossly unfair to his former wife.'

Moira Reynolds asked Dr Brown if he thought Leonora had narcissistic personality disorder.

'In my opinion, no. It's more likely that Sam Davison might have. He exhibited many of the characteristics of narcissists. He behaved with extreme selfishness before, during and after the divorce. Narcissists only consider others as part of their lives, as being available to satisfy their needs and desires. If they no longer do that, they are expendable. It's essential that the unfaithful partner takes responsibility for their actions, acknowledges the harm they've done. But someone with narcissistic personality disorder could not do that. Sam Davison never did.'

It illustrated the truth of the legal maxim, 'Never ask a question you don't know the answer to.'

Then came an expert on domestic violence: Sue Parkinson was a pretty brunette woman in her early forties. She had a PhD in psychology. She talked about how the kind of violence that occurs in the domestic sphere may not be physical but can sporadically be physical while mainly being psychological. Both are incredibly destructive.

'A woman comes to feel like a captive if she's in an abusive relationship and interestingly the pattern of behaviour is astoundingly predictable, once you've talked to enough women who've been abused by their intimate partners. The same technique was used on American prisoners of war in North Korea to cause them to defect to Communist China,' she told the silent courtroom.

Reynolds threw a look of disbelief in Rabinowitz's direction. He ignored it.

'They used what they call the three Ds: dependency, debility and dread,' Parkinson said. 'That is what an abusive man uses on the woman he wants to control. It's brainwashing and it's extremely effective. This is the answer to the question, why doesn't she leave?'

Rabinowitz asked Parkinson to explain more precisely what she meant.

'Violence only needs to occur occasionally for a woman to dread it. The threat of violence is much more effective in controlling a woman than actual violence. Dependency occurs because he cuts her off from family and friends and often refuses to allow her to work. Even when she does work, he is in total control of any money she earns. Debility is caused by emotional exhaustion because of the stress and trauma of the relationship.'

'Objection,' Reynolds's voice rang out. 'There is no evidence the accused was physically abused by her husband.'

'She hid the bruises and the abuse from her children and she hid it from most people, your honour,' said Rabinowitz. 'Only her closest women friends ever saw her with bruises and, as one has testified, a black eye. There is the photo of the accused with a black eye, said by the prosecution to be fake. There is also the testimony of Davison's work colleague who told police he was told by Dr Davison that he had beaten Leonora for being,' he consulted his papers, 'a mediocrity.'

There was a stir like leaves moving in a breeze in the courtroom. Justice White decided he would allow the expert evidence and Rabinowitz continued to question Parkinson.

Three of Leonora's friends met Tom Perry for coffee and told him what they had observed.

One of them, Meryl Thompson, told him that Leonora saw herself not only as Sam's victim but as a victim of the legal system. 'Over time,' she said, 'there was a loss of control, a loss of self-esteem and there was depression and anger and acting out.'

Amanda Coutts also saw changes. 'She ate a lot, she got fat and she didn't care how she looked any more – that made me sad. It wasn't like her at all. She was always very aware of her appearance, such a fashionista, but now she bought clothes and never wore them. They were hanging in her cupboard with the price tags still on them.'

Emily Fraser had known Leonora for twenty years. She called her 'a wonderful mother' and said she often let her babysit her baby son. 'I trusted her with him. Completely trusted her.' Emily had also put her husband through medical school. She worked while he studied. She understood Leonora's lust for jewellery and clothes. 'It's such a long grind and it's a struggle. Once the money starts rolling in, you feel you deserve nice things. You feel you've earned them.'

All three said they usually saw Leonora in tennis shoes and tracksuits rather than the designer dresses the prosecution referred to in their bid to brand her a 'socialite'. All three said Leonora didn't swear around them but Emily Fraser recalled her becoming incredibly frustrated when she couldn't get through on the phone to her children at Sam's house.

Two other women friends, Joy Taylor and Fiona Walsh, also met Tom Perry and told him that they had seen Leonora with a black eye and bruises. Leonora's housekeeper, Sarah Ryan, told Perry that Leonora was only happy around her children and when they weren't with her and were at Sam's, she spent most of her time crying. The picture they painted was one of an emotionally devastated woman who never had a chance to recover her equilibrium because Sam was so intent on destabilising her during one of the most vulnerable periods of her life.

Ellen Brown testified in court about the frantic phone call Leonora made to her after she fired the shots and fled the house. '"I think I fired the gun, it was dark in the room. I don't know if I hit anyone," she told me. She was sobbing and at one point it sounded as if she was vomiting.'

They met later and Ellen, who said Leonora had been very depressed for months, saw that Leonora was now in a devastated state, the like of which she had never seen her in before. 'Physically she was there but she was a husk, hollowed out.'

The marriage counsellor they had seen in 1976, Geofrey Plant, told Tom Perry that Leonora told him that on many occasions Sam had arrived home drunk and forced her to have sex.

Perry also talked to some of Leonora's family members. They also gave him examples of Sam's violent and abusive treatment of Leonora. These included 'choking her' and 'calling her names'. The names included 'silly', 'crazy' and 'stupid' and the sentence usually ended in 'bitch'. All of this had happened before they married, while they were still dating, they told Perry. Several of them testified to the court, too, on the violence and denigration Leonora had endured for years.

For Plant, Leonora was a classic battered wife. She told him sometimes she had to miss social events because she had a black eye and bruises. Plant also testified and ended his testimony by saying that Sam's actions had in his opinion pushed an already emotionally fragile woman over the edge into what the outside world would see as 'craziness'. Plant also claimed Leonora herself was in denial. One of the first things she had said to him was 'I am not a battered wife.'

'I did not agree with that,' Plant told the court.

Ben Nolan was Leonora's secret lover. She denied it for quite a while but eventually she caved and admitted to Tom Perry that, yes, he was in fact her lover. Tall and blond, and with his own construction company, he was the ideal new partner for her. She met him a year after the divorce came through. He was handsome, well-off and a perfect replacement for Sam. But for Leonora there was no replacement for Sam. She was still emotionally stuck even while Ben stayed at her house for days at a time and shared her bed. Ben testified that in the two years he had been with her she had been depressed 'almost all the time'. Leonora liked to spend a lot of time alone, was hypersensitive and suffered from insomnia, he said.

In her closing statement, Moira Reynolds rejected the idea that Leonora had acted spontaneously but maintained instead that she went to the house to kill Sam, that she had planned to do it, hence the gun she took with her. She killed out of rage and jealousy: rage at Sam for his infidelity and jealousy of the younger, more attractive woman he had married. Largely, she was motivated by hate, Reynolds said. Hate made her pull that trigger, not pain and not depression. Not despair. Her cry of 'I didn't mean to do it' simply did not wash. If she had no intention to kill, why take the gun and why fire it five times?

Hours passed, various jurors slept and woke, slept and woke and then Reynolds closed with these words, 'She went to that house on a killing mission and I ask you, ladies and gentlemen of the jury, to find Leonora Davison guilty of first-degree murder.'

Rabinowitz, naturally, did not agree. Leonora Davison was out of control, adrift in life, with legal documents flying at her while Sam simply refused to speak to her, Rabinowitz told the jury. Speaking to her would have eased the tension and allowed her to express her rage in a benign way. But Sam was determined that would never happen. In effect, he had placed his hand over her mouth and silenced her. When she eventually did speak to him and Susan, it was with a gun.

'The gun did the talking. Sam was cruel to her, unnecessarily cruel, and refused to take responsibility for the fact that he had betrayed her with Susan. That enraged Leonora and that rage had no safe outlet.'

Closing arguments took all day. It was 15 November 1993. One year after Leonora had fired five shots in that bedroom. The jury now had to consider the evidence and reach a verdict. The judge, Michael White, was a moderate man. He instructed the jurors on points of law and told them the idea of self-defence was not allowed. They could not even consider it because the murder appeared planned and the victims were asleep and unarmed when she entered the bedroom.

Leonora had arrived in court in a black dress with pearls at her throat.

At the end of the day, the jury retired and for five days there was no verdict. All the evidence and all the testimonies were considered before they eventually emerged to tell the judge they could not reach a verdict. White announced a mistrial.

'Shit,' pronounced Sam's friend, Kevin. 'I don't believe it.'

There was quite a flutter in the courtroom and then a strange, tense silence while everyone tried to take it in and some spectators wondered out loud what it actually meant. Leonora's daughters, Cecilia and Clare, burst into tears and photos of their tear-streaked faces were on the front page of every newspaper in the country next morning.

Ben: February 1992

Ben Nolan didn't see Leonora as a criminal because he fell in love with her as soon as he saw her. She was walking on the beach and he was jogging, as he did every morning. Sometimes, he finished his jog with a plunge in the ocean. She didn't normally walk on that beach so he had never seen her before. She noticed him and he noticed her noticing him. He was tall, muscular and fair-haired. She normally didn't go for blonds but she thought he was attractive and could see he was staring at her. She hadn't had sex for quite a while – except for the sex she gave herself – so when he stopped running and asked her the time, which was a transparent ploy to speak to her, she played along. Then, after some chat ,he asked if she would like a coffee and they walked back along the beach to a coffee shop called Beach Nook. It was full of all kinds of bright, colourful and expensive knick-knacks that people with too much money would buy, the way bowerbirds collect items for a nest. It smelled deliciously of coffee and bacon and eggs as they walked in the door.

Leonora sat at a table and the man she now knew was called Ben (he even gave her his business card with his website and his mobile number on it) went up to the counter to order their coffees. Skinny latte for her and a cappuccino with double shot for him. He also ordered breakfast for himself – a big breakfast with sausages, eggs, tomatoes and mushrooms.

'I don't know how you stay in shape,' she laughed when she heard his order.

'I work out,' he grinned, as if that explained everything.

Leonora studied his muscular body from the back. Nice legs. Nice arse. Of course. He worked out. But later she understood that he had worked physically hard most of his life, as a builder's apprentice and then as a builder himself. He was handsome in a fair-haired, easy-on-the-eye way and his body was pretty much perfect. Why he was interested in her was a mystery, she thought, pulling her pink T-shirt down over her slightly protruding stomach and tidying her hair with her hands.

He came back and sat down, smiling at her. 'Saturday,' he said cheerfully. 'I don't work today.'

Was this an invitation? Would he ask her out? And what would she say? She had no idea.

After coffee and his big breakfast, he asked her back to his beach 'shack' further up the beach. She had mentioned that she liked jazz.

'I love jazz! I've got a huge collection – on vinyl,' he enthused.

Leonora had a feeling he was younger than her, not by much, maybe five years. He suggested wine and jazz. She accepted and let the day take her where it would. She had nothing to go home to but an empty house, anyway.

The 'shack' turned out to be a beautiful double-storey house, right on the beach. Ben was clearly no pauper. They listened to them all – Mingus, Miles Davis, Coltrane – and then at some point, full of wine and jazz, she was naked in his bed and he was giving her sex and making her feel alive again. He was lovely, gentle but powerful at the same time, and she responded with power of her own.

If only it had been enough. If only she could have fallen in love with him the way he did with her. Instead, she let him live with her from time to time, let him be her lover, but her obsession with Sam continued like a sickness for which there was no cure. Ben satisfied her in bed, was handsome, kind and mad about her. He was even wealthy; though increasingly, that no longer mattered to her. She had seen the limitations of wealth, experienced its failure as a source of happiness. Ben was divorced and the father of two teenage sons. He understood her pain but not her obsession. He was a very different person.

Sometimes, she would wake with him touching and kissing her and they would roll together as if they had been doing it all their lives. Even when they hardly knew each other, she felt as if she had known him for a long time.

'I think I knew you in another life,' she told him one night when they had just had sex.

He laughed and kissed the back of her neck. If only she had met him instead of Sam all those years ago. Maybe they could have had a happy marriage but what good did it do to think like that? She had made her choice – for better or worse.

She woke and said, 'What are you doing?' even though she knew perfectly well.

'Playing with your beautiful arse. It's not illegal, is it?'

She laughed and let him play. She thought it was big and he thought it was beautiful. She was happy to concede. He was almost perfect and she was not.

She still thought about Sam day and night, hating Susan Davison, as she now was, and wanting the pain to stop. Ben couldn't stop it – he could only make her forget about it for a while. She was grateful but it wasn't enough to stop her steady progress down the path to destruction.

One night, she dreamed she was standing in the ruins of her beautiful house. The one where her children had been babies. The one she tried to burn down. In the dream, she had succeeded and shattered glass cracked and tinkled under her feet as she walked. Her mother appeared and said, 'You should have phoned me. I would've helped you.' Her smile was sad.

Leonora woke sobbing and Ben tried to comfort her. She slept in his arms that night but nothing he did or said could take away the sorrow.

Cake Eating

Leonora told herself, 'It's just a question of willpower and I have lots of willpower.'

She had weighed herself for the first time in years. She was eighty kilos. She was supposed to be between fifty and sixty kilos for her height, so she decided she had to lose weight. Only the day before she made this decision she had climbed on Ben for sex and realised that she was crushing him. When she leaned on his chest to steady herself, he laughingly said, 'Ouch, that hurts.'

Something had to be done. Since there was no way she could stop eating, especially the sweet things she loved, she would have to purge. Vomiting. She had done it before her wedding and had lost ten kilos. She was a slender vision in her wedding dress. 'A beautiful, glowing model of feminine perfection,' as her mother put it. Leonora smiled to herself. Well, of course she would say that. She was her mother. Now, she believed that the vomiting was an attempt to either deny or fix what was wrong with Sam. It stunned her that she had begun trying to fix him that early.

Her determination to lose weight when she was with Ben set up a cycle of gorging and vomiting that went on for a month or so. At first, she looked ill but she soon adjusted. She didn't need cake and chocolate quite so much now that she was having sex regularly with Ben but she didn't want to give them up either. As usual, she wanted it all.

When Ben went out for any reason, she would go to her stash. She had chocolates, cupcakes, Tim Tams and marshmallows hidden in a cupboard in her study. She would eat until she couldn't fit any more in, then – reeling with nausea and shame – she would go to the toilet and vomit until her stomach was empty. Ben knew nothing about it.

She would shower and clean her teeth as soon as she had vomited. Apart from a slight burning feeling in her throat from the stomach acid, it was as if the gorging had never happened. The results were immediate. Kilos dropped off her and soon she was able to take some of those clothes with the price tags still on them off the hangers and wear them.

Ben noticed the weight loss. 'Are you eating enough, sweetie?' he asked, running his eyes up and down her body.

'Of course I am,' she said edgily. 'You know I never met food I didn't like.'

He laughed and put his arms around her. 'You're getting skinny,' he said. But he didn't seem to mind too much. He might have, had he known that she was vomiting most of what she ate back up.

Soon, she was tired all the time. When Ben wanted sex (she didn't long for it any more, she was too tired), she was indifferent.

He would say, 'What's wrong, sweetie,' and do all the things she loved, sucking her breasts, stroking her clitoris, caressing her arse, kissing her passionately… 'What's wrong?' He would look upset, stare at her trying to work it out until she couldn't stand it.

'Come here,' she would say and he would roll against her and continue foreplay until she pulled him on top of her. Soon, she would be aroused: but it took longer to come. She loved being close to him, being held, but losing all that weight was defeating the purpose of losing it: to be more nimble and less heavy on top of him when they had sex. What use was it if her sex drive tanked?

After a month of low sex drive, she gave up, stopped vomiting but still watched carefully everything she ate. By the time she was arrested for murder, she was a nice weight. She was glad she wouldn't be photographed in handcuffs looking fat. Later she realised how dumb that was. What difference did it make? Only that she thought it might make her seem a less pathetic person – more in control.

Two days before the murder and her swift arrest, Ben had told her she looked lovely, perfect, and kissed her breasts. Sam would never have said anything like that to her. From the very beginning, she got nothing but put-downs. And worst of all, she thought he was very masculine, even sexy, when he disrespected her. She still did. She remembered him treating her with total disrespect and her looking at him and thinking, 'Well, at least he's a man.' So stupid – she could see that now. Why did she still go on loving him? Why could she not get free of her obsession with him and love Ben? He was so much better for her. If she could have loved him, it probably would have saved two people's lives. But she found herself remembering domestic details of her life with Sam when she was washing up, when she was cooking, even when she was in bed with Ben. Even when Ben was inside her.

Sam was her sickness and she had no idea how to recover. Could it be true that she was brainwashed as that Parkinson woman said in court. She still believed Sam was the one and that belief was her prison. Often she fell asleep at night cuddled up to Ben, her hand around his penis, her head nuzzled into his shoulder just above his bulging bicep.

He loved that. 'Good night, lovely,' he would say.

Even then, even in such moments, she would be obsessing over Sam and hating Susan. Fear would be gnawing at her insides. Fear that, between them, the love and the hate would destroy her: make her do something terrible.

Convenient Truths

Darren Rabinowitz was sitting at his desk feeling quite depressed and going through his case notes. He didn't believe the second jury would find Leonora not guilty. The mistrial was a bit of luck but he didn't really believe in luck. Then the receptionist came in and said there was a lady who wanted to see him. Her name was Alexa Nash.

'What's it about? Did she say?'

'She says she has some information on the Davison matter,' the receptionist told him.

Intrigued, Rabinowitz said, 'Send her in. I can see her now.'

Alexa Nash was tall and strikingly beautiful. She reminded him of someone. It was only later that he realised it was her father, who was someone he knew, casually. A tall, handsome politician – or had been; he had left politics. It was the name Nash that confused him, because that was her married name. The politician's name was Tate.

She strode in and held out her hand. He shook it and said, 'Darren Rabinowitz,' and she said, 'Alexa Nash.'

'Please sit down,' he said, indicating a chair near his desk.

'I want the jury to know what kind of man Sam Davison was,' she said.

Alexa Nash's blonde hair looked like a halo as the sun slanted in fiercely through the window and she certainly was potentially an angel for Leonora. Wistfully, he hoped she might be the breakthrough he was been waiting for.

'I was Sam Davison's lover when I was sixteen years old and he got me pregnant,' she told him. 'He forced me to have an abortion. It almost destroyed me. I want to testify. I think he was a sociopath.'

Rabinowitz leaned back in his chair, speechless. Not something he was used to. 'Heavens,' he said, with an ironic smile. She clearly knew next to nothing about the law, like most people.

'I've wanted to tell everyone about him for years. Now that my father's out of politics and I'm older and a married woman, it can't harm him any more. Sam Davison threatened me with the scandal. Said it would ruin my father's political career, but that's no longer true. There were other women too. Lots of them. He told me about some of them.'

Sam's friend Kevin's portrayal of Leonora as the devil and Sam as an angel would be blown apart by Alexa Nash's evidence – except that it was completely inadmissible. But still, Rabinowitz felt that exciting fizz in the belly that always meant good news for a case.

'I'm sorry, but no good judge would admit that evidence,' Rabinowitz told her regretfully.

'The law's an ass. And this proves it,' Alexa Tate laughed. 'I understand what you're saying. I feel sorry for the wife, that's all. He was the kind of man who would drive a saint to murder and from what I hear she was no saint.'

Rabinowitz said nothing. He was Leonora's defence counsel. There was nothing he could say. He showed her to the door and she flashed him an angelic smile as she left. How did a scumbag like Davison get his hands on these women? That's what he asked himself, going to the window to watch Alexa Nash striding up the street like a Nordic goddess and sliding into a Mercedes parked on the street.

As soon as she left, he was on the phone to his wife. 'You'll never guess what's happened!' he yelled into the phone.

'You sound excited,' she laughed.

'Of course you never really know which way a jury will jump but…'

'What do you mean?'

'I'll tell you all about it tonight.'

Rabinowitz hung up and went straight to the phone book looking for Alexa Nash's name. To his delight, he found that she had a number that was listed for a self-help group. A group for women who had had abortions. It was WHBA – Women Harmed by Abortion – of which

Alexa obviously considered herself to be one. He called the number and a woman named Tanya answered. He told her he was involved in a legal case and needed to do some research.

Which is how he found himself attending a meeting, accompanied by Lara, so that he wouldn't seem like some kind of male spy. The women were encouraged to sit in a circle on chairs and to share their deepest darkest secrets. He thought that probably people in their families and their closest friends might not have known what they shared at these meetings. Lara agreed with him later, when he mentioned it.

What interested him most was a comment from a woman called Maureen Harrigan who, it transpired, had also become pregnant to Sam Davison and had also had an abortion, though Davison had known nothing about it. She did it because she felt she would lose Sam if she did not.

After the meeting, there was tea and biscuits and both Alexa and Maureen came over to talk to Rabinowitz.

'Tell him what happened,' Alexa said.

'I thought I was in love with him and he acted as if he was in love with me. That was when I felt lower than zero. Knowing that I had had the abortion to hang on to him and all the time he was planning to dump me. He never cared about me at all. All he wanted was sex,' she said, looking heartbroken. 'I've had two children since but that only makes it worse in a way. When I look at them, I keep wondering what that baby would have looked like. I'm married now. But it's not happy ever after. I still struggle with what happened with Sam. I think I always will.'

Sam left a lot of wreckage in his wake.

Later, Rabinowitz went to the White Pages and found Maureen Harrigan's phone number. In the Yellow Pages, he even found an ad for her art gallery. She was beautiful too. Sam had definitely had a type. Young and beautiful. He was sure that both of these women could have a significant impact on the jury – but nothing they knew about Sam could be used as evidence. A judge would say it had no bearing on the case, because provocation was not an acceptable defence.

That night, he sipped a martini with dinner – a delicious spinach and feta pie made by Lara's own fair hands. She always made an effort on Friday nights, although through the week it could be hit and miss, and they always got the kids to bed early on Friday so they could have some together time, as Lara called it.

Darren told his wife that he thought he now knew how he could win the case. 'The guy was a total bastard,' he smiled. 'All that hero doctor stuff is garbage. He was a monster and these women would testify to that – if only they could.' He sighed. 'Maureen Harrigan says Sam was with hundreds of women and I'm willing to bet Leonora knows nothing about it.'

'So exciting!' Lara said, sipping white wine.

'I don't think Leonora will be excited. She thought the guy was a saint, at least until he left her for Susan. How do I get this information to the jury?'

'Don't they say there's more than one way to skin a cat,' Lara said with a wicked smile. 'You'll work it out.'

'Your faith in me is touching,' he grinned.

'And I've got a book you might like to read,' she told him. She put it on the table. 'You can read it tomorrow. I think you'll find it very interesting.'

He looked at the hardcover book. *Women's Shelters in Australia: A History* was the title in gold on a sky-blue cover. He looked mystified.

'There's a photo that I think you'll find absolutely fascinating,' teased Lara. 'But now that we've had dinner I need your attention in bed,' she purred, settling on his knee and kissing his neck.

'Really?' he laughed.

'Yes, I do. A woman has needs,' she said unbuttoning his shirt and taking his tie off.

She had a lot of needs that night and he was only too happy to supply them.

Around two in the morning, haunted by the blue book, he tiptoed out to the dining room, where it still sat on the table. He turned on a lamp. He could see that Lara had bookmarked a page, so he opened the book at that page and stared at the photo that took up all of the page.

'Some of the first volunteers to work at the new women's shelter,' read the caption. A sweet-faced blonde woman smiled at the camera. She looked tense. It was Sam's mother, Glenys Davison, who he had seen sitting like an avenging angel in court every day. Why would she be working in a women's shelter? Unless, he thought (suddenly realising what Lara was driving at), she had also experienced domestic violence. He went back to bed. And didn't sleep another wink.

The Do-over

There were two factors that loomed large in the retrial: malice and pre-meditation. The jurors from the first trial were asked for their opinions by Tom Perry in the hiatus before a new trial was confirmed.

Tim, twenty-seven, a mechanic, expressed the opinion that Leonora was provoked for seven years before she cracked. 'I feel like, what took her so long?'

Maria, thirty-nine, a sales assistant, insisted that only manslaughter was a just sentence, 'But we didn't have that option.' She didn't believe it was planned. 'She did it on impulse.'

Another juror who worked on aircraft engines for Qantas expressed what many jurors felt after listening to what Sam had put Leonora through. 'Only a saint could have taken what he dished out and not become violent.'

Both the defence and the prosecution were annoyed at the jury's inability to make a decision and deliver a verdict. Both lawyers would now be involved in the retrial. Rabinowitz was the defence in a fraud case and another murder trial in between Leonora's first and second trial. His house also burned down. It was not connected to any of his legal work.

'It was a hectic year. Very hectic,' he said with vast understatement. The changes he made for the second trial could be described as tweaking. He had had no idea that halfway through the trial, the equivalent of manna from heaven would walk into his office and change everything. 'The first trial was boots and all and then I had to find more boots,' he smiled as Tom Perry wrote it down.

Friends of the victims accused Rabinowitz of putting Sam and Susan on trial. But he disagreed. 'The victims are part of the story, part of the crime, they cannot be left out. It's all cause and effect. Everything is, when you think about it,' he asserted as Tom Perry took another slurp of coffee and wrestled with a ratty, stained notebook.

For her part, Moira Reynolds commented that the hung jury made her feel the system had malfunctioned. The system. Not her. Either way, she now had to saddle up and ride into battle once more.

Leonora held court in jail, visited by Tom Perry and eagerly telling her side of the story. She told him that it wasn't a revenge killing and it wasn't jealousy. 'I was never jealous of Susan in my life. I despised her, I had nothing but contempt for her.'

Then she posed for photos for the book, her hair newly blonded and bobbed and showing off her new slim figure.

'Everyone wants to see me as a woman who just wanted to kill a younger rival. How stupid is that? I never went to Sam's house intending to kill anyone.'

The newspapers published article after article suggesting exactly the opposite and even though there were plenty of photos around in which Leonora looked pretty, blonde and chic, they invariably used photos where she looked drab and crazed.

Perhaps unwisely, she compared jail to a holiday. 'After what I've been through, this is like a holiday resort,' she chirped. Even infractions of the rules that sent her to solitary were cause for rejoicing, she claimed. 'I love solitary. It's so quiet. I can read and I can exercise. I don't think the guards like it that I'm happy. They think I should be unhappy.'

Previously, after the separation and the divorce, she had been depressed, she told Perry. 'I felt as if alarms were going off in my head. Life was one long SOS. I wanted to save myself but I didn't know how. And the letters and legal documents never stopped.'

But jail was a doddle according to Leonora. 'There's no feeling of stress. No bills to be paid, no responsibilities. I can talk with other people or I can be alone. I write lots of letters.'

Eventually the new trial, the retrial began. Time passed. Weeks passed.

All the same information and the same witnesses were put before judge and jury. The jury this time was made up of eight women and four men. Justice Michael White presiding again.

Then, one hot afternoon in January 1994, Rabinowitz decided it was time to go for the jugular. Damn the torpedoes, full speed ahead. He called Leonora to the stand. She looked wary but pretty in a white cotton sundress and strappy pink sandals. She seemed composed; a hardened, battle-scarred veteran by this time.

Rabinowitz asked her a seemingly innocuous question. 'Mrs Davison, would you say you knew your husband well?'

Leonora frowned, then she laughed. 'Of course I did – for better or worse.'

There were some chuckles in the courtroom and the judge turned a frosty eye on the culprits, which silenced them.

'I wonder,' mused Rabinowitz, 'how well you really knew him. Because, you see, I have signed affidavits from fifty women who say he was their lover. During his marriage to you and after he married Susan Ross, too.'

Leonora's face fell, her mouth fell open into a perfect 'o', her hands went up to her face and then at some point she started to wail. It was a wail Rabinowitz had heard before. He had seen a documentary on grief and had heard a woman wail like it. In a war zone in some third world country, an ordinary looking, care-worn little woman had just been shown the mutilated body of her ten-year-old son. It was a wail of shock and incomprehension, of a grief too deep, too primal for words. The wail went on and on in the courtroom, high-pitched and tearing at the nerves of all who heard it. Rabinowitz noticed a couple of women jurors wiping tears away. And then, just as shockingly, the wailing stopped, filling the court room with a shattering silence. There wasn't a sound. Tom Perry scribbled like a man possessed in his notebook.

Leonora sat, mouth agape, very pale and wordless.

'Mrs Davison?' said Rabinowitz, not expecting an answer. He said it purely to emphasise Leonora's distraught state. The state she was in when she fired that gun, each and every juror would now be thinking. She also didn't correct him. In her mind, she was still Mrs Davison.

'Objection,' Moira Reynolds was on her feet. 'How is this relevant? And the prosecution hasn't seen these affidavits.'

Rabinowitz beckoned the clerk of the court over and he took copies of the affidavits and put them on Moira Reynolds's table. 'I only just received them, your honour,' he told the judge, 'an hour ago.'

'Mr Rabinowitz, you know better,' said the judge, not without a certain amount of admiration. 'The jury will disregard this evidence,' he said turning to the jurors. The judge then decided it was a good time to draw proceedings to a close for the day so that Leonora could recover.

Rabinowitz saw the look on Moira Reynolds's face. She was pale too, but with rage. As far as she was concerned, he had strayed into the territory of a dirty tricks campaign. She threw him a look of contempt as she gathered up her papers, including the affidavits, and walked out of the court. But the deed was done; the judge could tell the jury to disregard the question to Leonora and to disregard her response. He could even have it all struck from the record but Leonora's grief-stricken wailing was etched in the minds of everyone who heard it, especially the jurors. And she didn't even know about the pregnancies and the abortions.

Leonora was in shock and had to be helped from the courtroom by two policewoman. Tomorrow they would be back to Q & A with the witnesses, but this was a turning point. He could feel it.

Lara phoned him just as he reached the car. 'How did it go?'

'It worked but I may be disbarred,' he laughed.

'How did she take it?'

'Not well. Not well at all. It was pretty horrible, actually…'

The following day, one of the papers had an article with the headline, 'Red Terror'. Rabinowitz was a redhead and he had left his mark on all his children. The boy and both the girls were carrot tops. The article turned out to be a shonky, error-riddled summary of his career as a lawyer and depicted him as something of a wild man. Lara laughed so much reading it, he thought she would get a hernia.

What Rabinowitz would never forget was the look of pure hatred directed at him by Cecilia Davison as she left the courtroom. Clare was now a glamorous blonde, as much of a fashionista as her mother, while her sister Cecilia now favoured a simpler, classic style and had dyed her hair jet-black. Both girls had had their father's name 'Sam' tattooed on one shoulder. It was a small tattoo but Rabinowitz had seen it because of the dresses they were wearing in the hot weather. He wondered if those tattoos would now be removed. He realised for the first time when Cecilia looked at him like that, the full impact of what he had done. He had taken away their illusion that their father was a good man married to a difficult woman, a bitch. In a way, he had also taken away the illusion that they had had a happy family and a normal childhood. Was it any wonder Cecilia hated him? All of Sam's children probably hated him.

The next day, bright and early, they were at it again. To the surprise of spectators in the courtroom, Rabinowitz called Glenys Davison to the stand. She hated Rabinowitz and was in no mood to hide it. She glared at him as she took the oath. But Rabinowitz pitied her because now he suspected he knew her story.

After Mrs Davison had taken the oath, Rabinowitz took a deep breath and began. 'Mrs Davison, did your husband physically abuse you during your marriage?'

Glenys Davison went pale and swallowed several times.

Moira Reynolds was up at once, 'Objection. Relevance?'

'Your honour, this goes to whether or not Leonora Davison was abused, physically abused, by Dr Davison. There is ample evidence this kind of abuse can be learned by a child of an abusive marriage.'

Justice White gave Rabinowitz a slightly dubious look. He was frowning, but he said, 'I'll allow it.'

Glenys Davison stood silently. Then after a while she said, 'Yes, he did. But he got help for his anger and his drinking…'

'Did your son witness this abuse?'

Glenys Davison wiped away tears. 'Yes, he did. He would become very afraid: he was only a little boy and he would say, "Call the police." But I never did.'

Rabinowitz went cold. Call the police. The very thing Davison had said whenever Leonora would turn up at his house and want to talk to him. The last thing Davison said, according to Leonora, before she shot him.

'Call the police?' Rabinowitz mused. 'Was he physically abused by your husband?'

'No, it was just me. My husband would get like that because of stress, so I tried to create a low-stress environment.'

'And did that work?'

'Not really. All that helped was when he went for counselling and they told him to stop drinking because it was a trigger for his violence. He stopped drinking and the violence stopped.'

'How long did it go on for?'

'Sam would have been ten when my husband stopped drinking. When he was eleven, I had my daughter and a few months later my husband died of liver cancer.'

Not for the first time, Rabinowitz pondered why some people had such terrible luck in life. 'No further questions,' he said.

Moira Reynolds had no questions for Glenys Davison. This was a no-win situation for her.

Leonora was crying and the jurors looked restless. The judge called a short recess.

A Serpent's Tooth

How sharper than a serpent's tooth is an ungrateful child.

Shakespeare

'What do you remember about that day, Clare? The day your father died?' Tom Perry asked the teenage girl sitting across from him in his living room. She was a lovely-looking girl, blonde like her mother and like her – most of the time – fashionably dressed. Her dress was pink, short and elegant and it had a bow that sat prettily between her breasts. There were silver sandals on her feet and she had violet nail polish on her toes. She sat very still, thinking hard. Perry idly thought she looked a bit like Amanda Seyfried, the actress.

'I remember that we were at Nana's place,' she said.

'Your father's mother's place?'

'Yes. Susan and my father were going to go to the beach house they had bought at the coast, the next morning. That's what we were told but I noticed nothing was packed. Susan was a bit of a free spirit with those things. She would have packed about an hour before they left. But of course they never got to do that.' She stopped and looked down for a while. 'My father had bought his own boat, the *Suzy Q*, and they were supposed to be going out on the boat. Susan never really liked us coming along. She liked my father all to herself, I think, but she also was paranoid about one of us falling overboard. She didn't like having to watch us – even though we can all swim.'

'Go on,' Perry told her.

'Well, that's about it, until the next day when Nana came to pick us up from school and she was crying. She looked awful. Her face was grey and her eyes were red from crying. I tried to get her to tell me what

127 "

was wrong – I knew something was WRONG, SO WRONG – but she wouldn't tell me anything. Cecilia is kind of spooky, she knows things. I tell her she's got the sixth sense and she doesn't like me saying that. I never say it any more but I said it that afternoon when Nana came to pick us up.' Clare shivered briefly, crossing her arms over her chest.

'Why?'

'Because Cecilia knew. She said as soon as she saw Nana, Mum has killed them.'

'She knew your mother had killed your father and your step-mother?'

'Yes. She said it straight away and then she rushed over behind some bushes and threw up. As I said, she's very spooky that way. She's always been like that but she tries not to let her friends know because they'd tease her.'

'I suppose the trial has been very difficult for you. Were you sur-prised or shocked to hear that your father had been involved with so many other women?'

'I don't believe all that crap,' she said, coldly. 'I know my father and the man those women talk about is not my father, as I knew him.'

'You believe all those women are lying?' Perry asked her. 'Why do you think they would do that? Do you think they might have been paid?' he went on, in a neutral tone.

Her pretty little forehead developed a frown.

Perry went on, 'I have no dog in this fight but I find it hard to be-lieve that close to two hundred women are all telling the same lie – for no perceivable advantage to them. That doesn't seem to make any sense: not to me anyway.' Then he said nothing and just gave her time.

'Two hundred?' she said scornfully. 'Isn't it fifty?'

'That's just the ones who were prepared a make a statement and sign an affidavit. The actual number is closer to two hundred, it could be even more…'

She looked shocked, went pale but quickly recovered. Perry could see the walls she had built around the love she felt for her father going back up, one by one.

'So you say,' she said with a brief but cynical smile.

She was a tough girl and it wasn't surprising. What she had been through made you tough or destroyed you. She was not destroyed.

'How do you feel about your mother?'

'I hate her. She's wrecked our lives. None of us will ever be the same again.'

'You don't think your father provoked her into acting as she did?'

'I think she was a spoilt princess who was used to getting her own way and having anything she wanted. Her life had gone that way until my father left her and she just couldn't stand losing the marriage and the lifestyle. We lived very well. I only realise now because I'm not a child any more, how well we lived and how lucky and well, I suppose, privileged we were. My mother had that all her life and she couldn't cope with losing it, with losing my father. She was always really proud of the fact that a handsome doctor was her husband and she loved throwing those charity balls and playing Queen Bee. She told me once, "Without your father I'm only half alive." She was crying and I felt sorry for her at the time but now…now I just hate her. She didn't need to kill him. She took my father away from me. Now he'll never see me become a woman, get married, have children. He'll never be a grandfather – and I know how much he would have hated being a grandfather!' She laughed, but there were tears in her eyes.

'How are things with Antonella Morelli? Your other grandmother?'

'She's always idolised my mother. She never liked my father either, so you can imagine where she stands on all this.'

'She blames your father?'

'Yes, she blames my father for getting murdered because it makes her daughter look bad. It's crazy. I can't talk to her about any of it, so I don't see her much any more.'

'Does that make you sad?'

'Of course. She's my grandmother and I still love her.' She gave a comical little shrug, pulled an exasperated face. 'Growing up, I never expected any of this. Yes, they were not always happy and sometimes they fought horribly but I thought we were just like any other family. Parents fight, it's normal. But Susan, the divorce and all of that and then my mother murdering my father. I could never have imagined such a thing. Some days, I wake up and think it was all a dream. Or a nightmare,' she smiled, but it was a sad, weary smile.

'You experienced things a child never should,' Perry said.

'Yes,' she nodded. 'That's right. And I have to live with all of that and the murder of my father, every single day of my life. I can't un-know it. And of course it has destroyed my relationship with my mother and my grandmother but not with Nana. She's still there for me. And we siblings are still close, even though we don't agree on everything about the murder of my father.'

Perry's notebook was almost full, only a couple of empty pages at the back. Once again, it was brought home to him that in a murder there are many victims apart from the murder victim. Entire families can be devastated.

'Thank you for your time, Clare,' Perry told the girl. 'I really appreciate it.'

'I just want you to tell the truth in your book,' Clare said as they shook hands.

She left and Perry was sitting there thinking about how impossible it was to tell the truth. There were so many versions of the truth.

Perry arranged to meet Cecilia, the younger sister, in a coffee shop. She insisted that she wanted to meet him in a public place, which made him feel like a predator.

'Picking over the bones of a murder,' his girlfriend called it.

'It's my job,' he told her with a carefree grin.

'You're an undertaker,' she said. She always exaggerated and had a real flair for the dramatic.

He sat in the coffeeshop for half an hour waiting. He started to think Cecilia had chickened out but then he spotted her walking down the street dressed in a dramatic, short, purple kimono over a black dress. She was tall, slender and wearing very high black stiletto heels – all of this, combined with her jet-black bob, pale skin and very dark sunglasses made her look like a model. The Davisons made beautiful babies. Cecilia had grown up fast – she had to.

'Hello, I'm sorry I'm a bit late,' she said, sliding on to one of the white wicker chairs the coffee shop favoured as part of its black and white colour scheme.

'Oh, that's fine. Gave me time to get my notes in order,' he said laughing as he opened a new notebook.

Cecilia didn't laugh. She was a serious girl, on a serious mission. He couldn't see the tattoo on her shoulder that said 'Sam' but her allegiance was crystal clear. He had no illusions on that score. The girls had vetoed him talking to the boys. They told him they were far too young to be dragged into the book he was writing. In a way, they were on the path to being orphans and the girls were going to look out for their brothers. They had probably been doing that for a while.

'What do you remember about the day your father died?' Perry asked her.

'He didn't die, he was murdered,' she said, looking him right in the eye. 'Some people seem a bit confused. They say he died and how his death must have affected us and it makes me so angry. He didn't just die. He didn't have a heart attack or something, he was murdered. Shot four times.'

Her anger shocked him. He expected grief but not this burning rage. 'Of course. That's right,' he paused, uncertain what to say. 'So what do you remember about that day?'

'It was the worst day of my life.'

Christ. This wasn't going to be easy. Clare had been a walk in the park by comparison.

'I knew as soon as I saw Nana that Mum had killed them. She had threatened to do it often enough. She TOLD us she was going to kill them. She even said she was going to shoot them. I knew when I saw Nana that she had done it.'

'And how do you feel about your mother now?'

'I loathe her, of course. If there's a hell, I hope she goes there.'

Perry was so taken aback he was silent for some time.

'Do you think your father treated her badly?'

'A lot of women get treated badly and I suppose from her perspective she was treated badly but did he deserve to die? Absolutely not. She took our father away from us because she was jealous of Susan and couldn't stand for them to be happy when she was so miserable.'

Out of the mouths of babes. Now he understood why Rabinowitz had not called either of the girls to the witness stand in the second trial. The mistrial had only intensified their rage.

'I mean, come on. What gives her the right? If she had behaved like a normal person instead of a lunatic, her and my father could have come to a reasonable arrangement, but she didn't want that. She wanted him back and that was never going to happen. When she finally understood that, that's when she killed him. She was even sleeping with another man herself. Why not just let Dad go? Why do such a horrible thing? She's got a screw loose, sure, but I don't care. All I can think about is how afraid my father and Susan must have been and how she just left my father there to die. He wasn't dead, you know. They say he lived for half an hour. She could have called an ambulance but she didn't. She stole his wallet, though. Doesn't that tell you everything you need to know about her character? She told me that herself. Said she was ashamed.'

Perry couldn't imagine what kind of horrors went through this girl's head at night alone in her bed. If she was alone. She looked experienced. Lord only knows what kind of courage it took for a man to bed her. To bed either of them. Leonora's steely resolve was mirrored in them. They would always be her daughters no matter how much they hated her.

'Do you believe he beat your mother, as she has described?'

'Where's the evidence? There is none. And I never saw her with so much as a bruise.'

'She says she covered them with make-up. She didn't want you to know.'

'I've seen my father pull a drowning spider out of a bucket of water. He was not a violent person. Anyway, it's too late for her to play the caring mother now. That's all I have to say on the subject.'

The waitress brought their coffee. Cecilia had ordered decaffeinated.

'I'm highly strung,' she offered by way of explanation – with a shrug. So was her mother.

I Should Have Fucked Them All

Leonora sat in her cell staring at the ceiling, as Kay Tait read a women's magazine and ate an orange. Kay was reading about some actress's divorce. Leonora was thinking about men. All the men she could have had if she hadn't been such a dope as to believe in fidelity: to think it made her a good woman, to think that Sam was faithful until he met Susan. None of it was true. The scales had fallen from her eyes. She might never marry Ben Nolan. She wondered if she could ever trust a man enough to marry again. If she got out of jail, would she live as a free woman, free to bed who she chose and as many as she chose? If Sam had taught her anything, it was that the supposed virtue in being faithful was a myth. What did it give you? The ability to lie in bed at night feeling superior? Feeling like a saint? To hell with that. She thought she had only thought it but she had actually said it out loud, causing Kay Tait to look at her with a mischievous grin.

'To hell with what?' she asked.

'Never mind,' Leonora said.

'Oh, come on, Leo, you know I take an interest in what's goin' on with you.' She laughed a gritty, whisky drinker's laugh.

'I'm just thinking about what a load of bullshit I was taught by the church. That being a good girl and being faithful would make me a good woman who deserved a good man.'

'A good man?' Kay Tait snorted as if she had never heard of such a thing.

'I know it's no good talking to you. You think all men are bad.'

'The ones I knew were. Every single one of 'em,' she said, going back to her magazine. 'Drunks, drug addicts, serial cheaters, pornographers – not that I don't enjoy a good bit of pornography as much as the next girl – kiddie fiddlers. Christ, I had 'em all. The dregs of humanity. Is it any wonder I killed one of them?' She sniggered and said, 'Look at this. They say this movie star, silly bitch, married this guy and left him three days later. She ran off with a WOMAN. They don't know they're alive. Oversexed and overpaid.'

Leonora couldn't help laughing. When Kay got wound up, she was funnier than any stand-up comedian.

'As far as I'm concerned,' she went on, 'the only thing that makes a man worth my time at all is that he's got a penis. The bigger the better. I can't be doin' without that.'

Leonora giggled and Kay put the magazine to one side. 'Don't you agree? What else are they good for? They have guns and they have wars because they can never be satisfied with the size of their penis. They always want a bigger weapon. Don't they?'

Leonora was laughing now, a great big belly laugh.

'You know I'm right, Leo. Don't you?'

'It'll be lights out soon. If you want to read that story about the movie star, you better hurry up and stop talking funny stuff to me.'

'I'm ready for sleep anyway, babe,' Kay told Leonora, climbing on to her bunk, the top bunk.

Leonora pulled back the covers and got on her bunk too. Within seconds, the lights went out and another night in prison began for both of them.

Leonora started going over in her mind all the men she could have had and what she would have liked to do with them. Not only did it give her an enjoyable throbbing sensation in her pussy, but it transported her out of the prison into a fantasy world where she could have any man she wanted and do whatever she liked with him.

Graham Toltu – a truly gorgeous black boy she had met at an interschool dance. He was so beautiful, like a black Adonis with a muscular body and a big, sweet smile. Now that was truly a wasted opportunity. She pictured herself naked in bed with him and how she would kiss him all over and kiss between his legs and lick his nipples. He would quickly be on top of her giving her what she wanted.

Her hand went between her legs and she concentrated on being very quiet, even though she soon heard Kay snoring as she did every night. Like an overloaded freight train going up an incline.

As her fingers got busy, she remembered Ken Corbett, a real blond beauty who had taken her to the pictures and put his hand down her blouse to play with her breasts and stroked and squeezed her nipples until she had to take a deep breath to stop herself moaning with pleasure. Ken and her were on a tropical island out in the middle of a rainforest. There was no one around for miles. He was very tall, about six feet two, and powerfully built. There was an infinity pool and a two-room cabin.

Kay stopped snoring and turned over in bed, causing Leonora to freeze but soon she could hear her heavy adenoidal breathing again.

Back in the rainforest, Ken was naked and had an erection you could break a plate on. She was naked too and then they were fucking by the infinity pool. Her hand moved faster and faster.

Greg Deems – he was not all that tall, about five nine, but he was the sexiest boy she had ever seen. Brown hair and blue eyes and luscious lips, pouty and red. He was nineteen when she knew him, from another nouveau riche family. His father owned a plumbing business, which was pretty much a license to print money. He took her out for a while, driving her around in his white sports car, until he realized she would never give him sex.

Her hand slid up and down on her clitoris. What a fool she had been. She had feared pregnancy as well as the shame of being found out by her parents. She knew orgasm was close now and she and Greg were in a hotel room on a big bed with crisp white sheets and a view over the lights of the city. It didn't matter which city, it was a fantasy city anyway. Greg was sucking her breasts and fingering her clitoris. His big stiff penis was pressing against her thigh. His darkly tanned body was so beautiful against the white sheets that she had to kiss it and then he grabbed her head and put his tongue in her mouth and as he did, Leonora came fiercely, for a long time. As she did so, she buried her face in the pillow so she wouldn't make a noise and wake Kay up. Breathless, she turned over with her hand between her legs and enjoyed the contractions that followed the orgasm.

While she was in jail, she would get her thrills this way but if she got out, she would find men who could give her what she wanted. Being married to Sam had been an education and she didn't intend to waste that education ever again. She laughed softly in the dark, remembering how she had failed the test the nuns gave them on sex education. Given the chance, she would never fail it again.

Kay snored on but in spite of that, Leonora was soon fast asleep.

The next morning, Kay bought the newspaper at the canteen and gave it to Leonora to read. There was an article about the murder and about her trial but most of all about her. They couldn't say much about the murder or the trial and used the words 'alleged' and 'allegedly' a lot, but they could say a lot about her and they did.

'The usual hatchet job,' sneered Kay. 'But that's a nice photo of you. Love that dress.'

'It cost a lot of money. That photo's from the eighties,' murmured Leonora, reading the article at speed. 'That was at a charity dinner that was raising money for cancer research.'

'Oh well, excuse me, Lady Bountiful,' Kay laughed.

'I didn't mean it like that,' Leonora said, feeling a bit ashamed.

'That's okay, babe. You can't help it that your old man was rich,' Kay said with a grin. 'It didn't really do you all that much good, did it?'

'No, it didn't and the media has hated me from day one. They always write about me as if I'm Lizzie Borden – a crazed axe murderer. And they always like photos that make me look like a rich bitch, a heartless bubble head.'

'Don't worry, I know you're not that.'

'But a lot of people don't and articles like this won't help my case. I wish they would wait until the trial is over and then they can say whatever they like.'

'They just want money and your trial is good copy – and so are you.'

'That's no consolation,' Leonora said, eyes glued to the article.

'Honestly, the way they talk about you. It's nothin' like you at all,' Kay said.

'I know. It annoys the hell out of me. Aren't they supposed to inform the public? The idiots. All they do is lie and distort the facts.'

'They seem to think that's their job,' Kay snickered. 'You should have seen the things they wrote about me. Hangin' was too good for me, according to those bastards. I was the wicked fuckin' witch of the west.'

Leonora couldn't help laughing. 'So where's your broom?'

'Where's yours?'

They fell about laughing and one of the passing guards gave them a dirty look. Where was the repentance? Where was the remorse?

They waited until the tough-looking female guard was out of earshot and then Kay chanted, 'Cunty, cunty, cunt,' until Leonora collapsed in raucous cackles and laughed until there were tears in her eyes.

'I smell pig,' Kay added.

'Stop it! My stomach hurts,' Leonora said.

'I know you can smell it too. Oink, oink, oink…'

'You're crazy.'

'Yeah, tell me somethin' I don't know, babe. The papers said I was, too. Journalists make me hurl. Can I have that magazine again? I didn't finish readin' about the lesbian movie star. Every word of it is true. It's in a MAGAZINE,' she said, rolling her eyes and giggling.

'Davison, you wanted to make a call,' the guard said and Leonora went down the hall to take the phone call.

It was Ben. 'I miss you, baby,' he said.

'I miss you too. Well, certain parts of you,' Leonora said.

He laughed. 'You don't miss my wit and charm?'

'You know what I miss,' she said, laughing. She wasn't going to give him any romantic bullshit. It was what it was.

'Can I come and visit you?'

'No. I told you. I don't want you seeing me like I am in here.'

'I don't mind.'

'But I do.'

'Did you get the water bottle I sent you?' he asked in a mushy voice.

Poor bastard. He was in love with her.

'Yes. I always feel cold in here. I snuggle up to it and pretend it's you.'

It was partly true. He didn't need to know the full picture.

The Guerilla War Phase

Sitting in her cell, without even Kay Tait for company (she was at the dentist:escorted by guards) Leonora remembered when Sam moved to the guerrilla war phase. He had never been controlling – hostile, yes, but not controlling. Now suddenly he was. It happened in the space of twenty-four hours; he became alpha maledom in all its dubious glory. The violence was random and always caught her off guard but once he had entered this new controlling phase it was constant. The random violence would descend out of nowhere and be over as quickly as it started, usually. Like the time she had Cecilia dressed to be baptised and Sam was furious that she was wearing a christening robe Antonella had bought. HE wanted to provide that robe because, he raved, she was HIS daughter. Leonora had no problem with the robe but it soon became clear she did have a problem with Sam.

'Why does she have to wear something your mother bought? I've got plenty of money.'

Leonora knew better than to say anything, but it didn't help. Soon they were rowing and while she stood there with the baby in her arms, he punched her in the face and her nose bled all over the christening robe – so that was that. It went in the bin. Her clothes were ruined, so they went in the bin too. She put the baby in the bassinet and stripped completely, then took a shower – only to find that he was standing in the doorway watching her and watching the watery blood run off her body with great appreciation. Almost with lust.

'You're sick,' she told him.

He grinned moronically and just went on watching.

In new clothes, with her bruises covered with make-up, the baby in another white outfit indicating her spotless soul (but then there's always original sin – we've all got that), they arrived at the church. Antonella noticed immediately that the baby was not in the christening robe and Leonora mouthed, 'Tell you later.' She never did and never would. A lie would have to be found. She couldn't remember what lie she had found. Antonella believed it. She wanted to believe it and she did. The baptism went to plan. It was a lovely, crisp, sunny winter's day. Everyone was happy and Leonora acted the role of the happy mother convincingly. No one suspected a thing.

When Leonora told Rabinowitz about this incident, he said, 'Witnesses?' and she shook her head.

Rabinowitz said, 'Hmmm,' which she now knew meant, 'Not a snowball's chance in hell.'

The violence was mostly in the mid-marriage era. The controlling hostility was in the late era of the marriage when he was already with Susan. Was it driven by guilt? No. Leonora had to admit that he never showed any signs of guilt. Never. No matter what he did. Not that the random violence ceased. It continued. But suddenly Sam was obsessed with who she was talking to on her phone, who she was going to the movies with, where she went when she left the house. It looked like jealousy, meaning sexual jealousy, but he never suffered from that – even when she was young and beautiful. No, it wasn't that: she decided that it was simply that he wanted power over her as a last triumph in a relationship where he had always had the power. And the more power he got, the more he wanted and the more he abused it. Even when he knew the marriage was over, or perhaps because of that, he decided to control everything she did. Did he suspect that she had a lover? He was wrong if that's what he thought. She had never been unfaithful. Fool that she was. Dr Parkinson was right about violence: she realised now that she had lived in fear of it, even though it only occurred randomly and infrequently. Most of all, she dreaded it happening in front of the children, but he was cunning to the last. The childen never saw or heard that side of him. He made sure they didn't.

A Life Misspent: Kay Tait's Misfortunes

Sometimes at night, before lights out, Kay and Leonora would lie on their bunks, drowsy but not yet ready to sleep, and talk about their lives. How they got where they were. Leonora suspected that Kay's story was pretty much unbeatable. She suspected her story could not compete with it and she suspected that there were very few women with a comparable tale to tell.

'I was chosen at birth,' Kay laughed in her husky, whisky-voiced way. 'Chosen to eat a shit sandwich where men were concerned. I just had the knack. If they put me in a room with twenty men, I would choose the one that would make me suffer. I had a gift!'

Leonora chuckled. 'You're so funny,' she told her.

'Listen,' Kay said. 'I'm not jokin'. I have a gift. It started with my father. He made me have sex with him until I was sixteen. Started when I was ten and went on until I was a teenager and completely out of control. I ran away from home then. He beat my mother and always told her she was ugly and stupid and no other man would even feed her if she left him. So she didn't. I never knew if she knew or suspected what he was doing. I only had a brother and, lucky for him, my father wasn't into boys, so it was just me.'

'I can never understand how these men don't know that what they're doing is wrong,' Leonora said, shocked and trying not to show it.

'I think he knew but he just didn't bloody care.'

'Was he religious?'

'Hell, no. He didn't believe in anything, including religion. My mother was quite religious, Catholic, and he mocked her constantly over it. One time, he caught her praying with some rosary beads. He grabbed them and whipped her across the face with them and when I started crying he whipped me too. He was a beast, an animal. I don't know how he got that way but, as soon as I could, I ran away from home. And then I just got mixed up with one bastard after the other. I was pretty then. Blonde, great tits, nice legs. You'd never know it now. Life has wrecked me. And all it got me was the attention of one arsehole after the other. There seemed to be somethin' in me that made them want me. Like I had a sign on my forehead that read "victim".' She laughed until she went into a coughing spasm. 'I'm tellin' ya, those mongrels couldn't get enough of me. They fucked me like it was a matter of urgency. As if fuckin' was going to cease to exist sometime soon.' She fell silent, remembering God knows what kind of things they did to her.

'Go on,' Leonora said. 'It's so interesting.'

'So interestin', is it, your ladyship? It wasn't bloody interestin' when it was happening to me,' she said, a bit angry. But then she went on. 'There was only three of them I cared about and they were the ones that treated me the worst. The first man I was ever with, after dear old dad, was Harry Fletcher. I was seventeen and he was twenty-four. He was a singer in a band and he was rotten to the core but how was I supposed to know? I didn't know anythin' about men, my father not bein' a reliable guide for what to look for in a man, and I thought he loved me and I thought I was in love with him. He was the most beautiful-lookin' man I had ever seen. He had blond curly hair and a face like a fuckin' angel and a body like a god. How was I supposed to know he was bad? He gave me weed to smoke and sometimes he gave me nice things and he held me in bed and made me feel good. I had never been held like that, I thought I was in heaven. He could be so kind, so funny, so lovin' and that was the person I fell in love with, but he needed to control everything I did and he always thought I was havin' sex with other guys. I wasn't but he never believed me and when he got jealous he would smack me around. After a year or so, the band got a recording contract and he and the rest of them just left for Melbourne. He never even told me. I found out from other people that he was gone. The pain of that nearly killed me – it was worse than giving birth. I got pregnant, of course, and they always made you give the baby away if they could. So I did. It was a little girl with blue eyes like his. I couldn't look after a baby. I could barely look after myself.'

'Don't feel bad about it. It wasn't your fault,' Leonora told her, gently.

'I don't. The kid was better off away from me. There were a lot of men then, different ones all the time because I thought if that's what love feels like, then I don't ever want to love anyone again. I started takin' the pill so I was safe from gettin' pregnant but I wasn't safe from lovin' another one of those bastards, was I? No, I wasn't. His name was Tom Hawker and he worked in a department store. He had black curly hair, brown eyes, he was tall and incredibly handsome. I fell madly in love with him. We would have sex in his car. He couldn't afford to take me out much, though we went to the pictures sometimes. It turned out he was actually married but I must have seemed like a better option in terms of findin' someone to victimise, so he left his wife. They had been savin' to buy a house and he took all the money and left her in the lurch. That should have told me everythin' I needed to know but I'm just a fuckin' fool for love, aren't I? We found a nice flat and could pay the bond because he had the savin's he'd taken. I felt a bit guilty about it but you know how ruthless young girls are. I wanted him and that was that. Soon we were short of cash and so he suggested I go on the game. I was too stupid to say no. He smacked me when I even looked reluctant, so I knew I had to do it. I was terrified he would leave me the way Harry did. I thought, I can't go through that pain again. This time it will kill me. It was horrible. I got to see the really depraved side of men, the things they did to me and the way they treated me…sometimes I think that's why I killed. I had so much rage in me because of what I had to do with those men. And he wouldn't let me stop. "We need the money," he would say. "You'll never earn this much doin' anything else." So I got trapped in that life and when I was fallin' apart because of it, Tom got me on heroin. That's what they do. Then you need the money to buy drugs and you're trapped. You go out on the street and you bring the money home and you give it to the man waitin' at home and he gives you heroin. He never even protected me, like some of them did. I was just out there on my own. Sometimes I hated him but mostly he only had to kiss me or call me darlin' and I was on my knees to him. You know that scar on my arm?'

'Yeah.'

'I got that from one of those animals, my "clients" as Hawker called them. He was a sailor, a drunken sailor,' here she laughed until she snorted. 'He smashed a bottle and slashed me with it. I crawled home to Hawker bleedin' like a stuck pig. He was really angry because he had to take me to the hospital to get stitches and I couldn't work for a week. I almost died because that shit slashed an artery and I could have bled to death. I had to have a blood transfusion. Hawker didn't care. I was just an inconvenience. That's when I woke up. I realised the only way I would leave Hawker was in a coffin and I decided that wasn't goin' to happen. He went out one night, probably fuckin' some other woman – who cares, Leo, who fuckin' cares – and I grabbed all my stuff and ran for it. I stole his stash of money too. He would have killed me if he caught up with me.'

Lights out. But they just lay there in the dark and Kay went on talking.

'I decided I needed a completely new start. So I went north and ended up on the coast in Tweed Heads. That's when I met the worst one of all. Not straight away. For about six months, I lived a normal life. I got off drugs, got a job in a café and had a nice little flat. I used to go to the beach in the mornin' and have a swim and then go to work. It was nice. The most peaceful time I ever had – because there was no man to knock me around or make me do things I didn't want to do. I liked my job in the café and my boss was nice. But it couldn't last. No. I met Talford Monroe. His friends called him "Tally" because he was six foot four and he only drank tallies. Good lookin' – for a drunk.' She went quiet. 'He could charm the birds off the trees when he was sober but when he was drunk he was a devil, I'm tellin' you, a devil is what he was. The things he did to me were pure evil and he was determined to go on doin' them, so he wouldn't let me go. If I tried to leave, he would put his hands around my throat and strangle me until I blacked out and then I would wake on the bed with the bedroom door locked and the clothes out of my suitcase thrown around the room. Then I'd tell myself, Better luck next time, and put my clothes away. He murdered some guy when he was drunk but no one knew except me, because he told me. Left him lyin' in an alley with his head bashed in. So then he decides we have to get married so I can't testify against him in court. My mother couldn't afford to come to the weddin' and I didn't want my father there so it was just Tally, me and a couple of his mates who were witnesses. It was all legal, though. He got weirder after that. Much weirder. He was obsessed with the idea the police either knew or would find out and that I would go and tell them so they'd lock him up and I'd be free of him. I was too scared to do any such thing. He'd always hit me but now there were full scale beatin's and I was convinced he wanted to kill me. I bought a knife one day when I was out, not really thinkin' I would ever use it. I mainly wanted it to scare him off if he was goin' to beat me. But in court they claimed it proved the killin' was premeditated. My lawyer was useless. I actually think he hated me and wanted me put away. So there was that,' she laughed bitterly.

'My lawyer is fighting very hard for me,' Leonora said quietly.

'Yeah, but you weren't a prostitute. You're a good girl. I was a former drug addict prostitute. My lawyer really didn't care what happened to me, that's a fact. They don't like a woman to fight back. If you're a victim and dead, you get more respect than if you kill the bastard.'

'Surely they understood that you had no choice,' Leonora asked her.

'Nah. They didn't. They said I planned it and that's true, I suppose, but I only planned it after he almost bashed me to death and told me he was goin' to kill me. If he hadn't passed out in a drunken stupor, I would have died that night. And once I started stabbin' him, I just couldn't stop. I was angry. In fact, I know now I've been angry most of my life, and all that anger came out as I stabbed him. They say I stabbed him twenty times. He was unconscious from drink. The prosecution argued I could just have left and didn't need to kill him. That's bullshit. If I hadn't killed him, sooner or later he would have killed me. I knew that. My lawyer said I would have to testify about what happened with my father or they wouldn't believe me. The prosecution tore me to shreds. After he was finished with me, I didn't even believe it happened. The jury didn't believe it either. I had no witnesses, only my word. And why would they believe a prostitute drug addict? My mother claims to this day she didn't know what my father was doing, so she couldn't testify – or wouldn't. So there you are. That's my sad story.'

'I don't think I'm going to be able to sleep tonight,' Leonora said in a shaky voice.

'Come on, Leo. We're tough. If you can't sleep, wake me up and I'll sing you a fuckin' lullaby,' and she laughed like a loon.

Laughter was the only thing that kept her sane. But Leonora knew a den of monsters lived in her head in spite of the laughter. How could they not?

Then she heard Kay say sleepily, 'Look at that fuckin' moon. Full moon. I always think it looks like a skull.'

Leonora felt cold all over thinking about that ten-year- old girl being raped by her father. Out there on a farm with no one to dry her tears. No one to help her.

'G'night, babe,' Kay mumbled.

'I'm sorry, Kay,' Leonora said. 'I'm sorry life treated you the way it did.'

But there was no answer and soon the snoring started. Something familiar. Something she could understand. Then she was asleep too.

The Mystery of the Rogue Male

'Did you ever hear about Musth? You know, when male elephants go crazy?' Kay Tait asked.

'No, I didn't,' Leonora laughed. 'Is it true? They go crazy?'

'Yeah, apparently. Suddenly, they have sixty times as much testosterone in their bodies as normal. When they're teenagers. Makes them mad. They get so aggressive they even attack rhinos…'

'Oh, stop it!' Leonora laughed like a loon. 'Stop it!'

'It's bloody true, I read it in a book I found in the library at Tweed Heads. I should have paid more attention. Men have twenty times as much testosterone in their bodies as women do. Did you know that?'

'No, I didn't.

'Well, it's true and it's only now I can see the connection.'

'What connection?'

'I was obviously always attracted to men with lots of testerone. And it makes men aggressive. Makes them crazy, like the elephants. That's why they beat me.'

'Well, I can tell you from experience, it's nothing you did. Because it didn't matter what I did, when Sam wanted to beat me, he did.'

Kay had tears in her eyes. 'Thanks, babe. I know that. I wish I'd known more about testosterone. I wish I'd known more about everything. Did you know that a survey found that globally, ninety-six per cent of murderers are male?' she added.

'I didn't, no.'

'So we're rare birds, aren't we?' Kay gave a nervous giggle.

'I suppose we are.'

'Freaks.'

'I wouldn't go that far,' Leonora said, alarmed at the course the conversation was taking.

'But we are, aren't we? Think about it. Ninety-six per cent means the "normal" murderer is almost always male. So that's why the jury thinks there must be somethin' terribly wrong with us,' Kay said, climbing up on to her bunk and lying down with her arms behind her head. 'Maybe there is.'

'You're not yourself, Kay. What's going on?'

'My daughter contacted me. She wants us to meet.'

'Well, isn't that fantastic? Isn't that a good thing?'

'Not if I'm a freak. I don't want to taint her, you know. I don't want to contaminate her.'

'Kay, you won't. You were in a bad place before but now you're…'

'In jail for first- degree murder, yeah. A great role model, aren't I?'

'She wants to see you, even though she knows all that. You should meet with her. Let her visit you.'

'I can't understand why she wants to see me. I abandoned her.'

'You did what you thought was best at the time. How old is she?'

'She'd be seventeen now.'

'Old enough to know if she wants to meet you or not.'

'I told her I had to think about it.'

'Don't wait too long. Haven't you two waited long enough to meet each other?'

Kay was crying and Leonora let her cry. One thing she had learned is that you think you have forever with your children, with your life, and then suddenly you don't have any time at all.

'Don't wait too long,' she told her again.

'She went lookin' for Harry but he, well…' her voice faltered. 'He died of a heroin overdose a few years ago. My beautiful Harry, already dead. I can't believe it.'

She climbed down from her bunk, collected her toiletries bag and a towel, fresh clothes, change of underwear. 'I'm going to have a shower. Clear my head.'

She pressed the buzzer, a guard came to the door and let her out and escorted her to the shower block. Half an hour later, a siren went off, which Leonora knew meant there was an 'incident' somewhere in the prison. Kay hadn't come back and Leonora immediately got the strangest feeling in her stomach. As if someone had punched her there.

Kay didn't come back and then the siren stopped. Around five in the afternoon, a guard came and told Leonora that Kay had been beaten up in the shower by another inmate. A half crazy woman in for drug offences, who was always spoiling for a fight had focused on Kay and attacked her.

Leonora felt sick. 'Is she okay?' she asked the guard.

'She'll live. Should be back in a day or two,' the guard told her. 'She's in the infirmary.'

In one of those ironies that life throws up so often, it was the guard who Kay had said 'Cunty, cunt, cunt' about.

Just as the guard had said, Kay appeared two days later, bloody but unbowed. Her face was a mess, she had two black eyes and cuts and grazes all around her mouth. The first thing she said was, 'It could have been worse.'

Leonora cried.

'I started to feel safe, that's why it happened,' Kay said.

'What do you mean?'

'I was goin' to meet my daughter and I could be up for parole in the next three years. There's someone somewhere who decides whenever things are goin' well for me, that can't be allowed. I started to feel safe and that wasn't allowed either. It's hard for someone like me to feel safe. Livin' hand to mouth, you never feel safe. I was off balance. That's why that crazy bitch singled me out.'

'Feeling safe is an illusion,' Leonora said. 'I convinced myself I was safe with my beautiful children, my handsome husband and all that money. But you know, I never was. All that time I was an abused wife and he was having sex with other women. They even say he was using drugs,' she rolled her eyes, 'et cetera, et cetera. I was living a lie and the money and all that stuff made no difference because one day it was like an angel with a sword flew down from heaven and cut my wealthy life, my fake heaven, to ribbons. And it could never be repaired.'

'But at least you had it to lose,' Kay insisted as the crack in her lip began to bleed. She grabbed a tissue and dabbed at it. 'I never had the big house, the cars and money in the bank. Never had that.'

'Well, it makes no difference, let me tell you. When that angel flies down, nothing and no one is spared. I don't even miss all that. What I miss is the illusion: having a family, a husband to look after me, children who love me. They hate me now because I killed their father and I've tried but I can't actually convince myself I don't deserve it. Meet with your daughter if there's any chance she might love you – it's the only thing that matters.'

'I can't let her see me like this anyway,' Kay laughed and then screeched with pain.

'No, you look scary. Tell her you can't see her for a couple of weeks. But don't miss the chance to know her. You'll regret it for the rest of your life.'

Leonora had dressed for court in a pale blue suit, a white silk blouse and a single string of small pearls and matching earrings. She wore the shoes she had worn to the charity garden party where Susan Ross turned up: white sandals with gold kitten heels. Then the guards were there and Leonora was handcuffed and taken to the van to be transported to the court; to face the eyes of the spectators, the words of her accusers and the humane logic of Rabinowitz. Between them, the truth was contested, strangled, suffocated, and sometimes lost.

Tripping

Jolting along in the van on the way to court, Leonora suddenly remembered a very strange trip she had taken with Sam shortly before he moved out. They had been brawling all day – over Susan, over Leonora's mothering skills, over who was the worst influence on the children. It was a nightmare and the kids would have heard it all if they hadn't been out. That weekend, they all had somewhere else to be. Clare was going to a movie with her friend Sacha. Cecilia was going to a sleep over with some girls from her class at school. Both Shane and Tom had been invited to birthday parties. Being alone in the house with Sam created a very sinister atmosphere.

'You know our marriage is over, Leonora. You must know that!'

'You're selfish! You only love yourself. I hope Susan Ross knows that.'

'Selfish! You are the most selfish person I've ever met,' yelled Sam.

And so on and on and on. It got louder and more vicious with each exchange of insults. Leonora sat at the kitchen table crying and Sam stood looking out a window with his back to her.

'Let's go for a drive. Then we can both calm down,' he said.

'What? Where to?'

'Into the country. Where it's peaceful,' he said smiling and acting charming. The way she hadn't seen him act in a very long time.

'Okay. I'll just grab a coat in case it turns cool,' she said, looking puzzled.

They got into the four-wheel drive and headed out of the suburbs and then out of the city. It was strange being alone together like that. So strange that Leonora kept glancing at Sam trying to read his face. It was completely inscrutable.

'Where are we going?' she said at last.

'Somewhere nice and quiet,' he said in a strange voice.

Where was he taking her? And why was he acting so strange? It was a complete turnaround from how he had been behaving since he met Susan Ross. Soon they were in a rural area. She was so distracted she hadn't looked at the signs on the side of the road. He drove the car deep into the bush and they came to a little stream running through bushland made up mainly of gum trees – ghost gums and eucalypts and also some scrubby wattle trees.

'What are we doing here?

'Good question, Leonora.' He hadn't said her name in so long that she burst into tears. 'How did we get here?'

'I still love you,' she told him sobbing. 'I don't think I can stop.'

He looked at her strangely and she noticed he was very pale. His hands were clenched into fists. 'You're going to have to, can't you understand that?'

'No, Sam. No. I don't want to.'

He exhaled as if a weight was lifted off him. 'You have to try. I love Susan…'

'No,' Leonora wailed, as if he was stabbing her. His words cut her.

He seemed to make a decision then. He shook his head and started the car, backed up and got back on the highway. They drove in silence for quite a while and then he suddenly sped up and started driving crazily.

'Maybe we should go together,' he said in a flat, dead voice; all emotion washed out of it.

'Go?' she said baffled.

'End it. Once and for all,' he said in that same zombie voice.

'Slow down!' she screamed. 'Slow down, please, Sam. Think of the children. What will happen to them?'

He turned and looked at her and she could see for the first time how much he hated her but in some strange way that knowledge could coexist with the fact that she loved him and would not ever stop. He slowed down, then, and drove to the cinema where he had to pick Clare and Sacha up. They drove Clare to Sacha's house, where she had decided she would spend the night. The two girls chattered and laughed in the back of the car but Sam never said another word.

Now on her way to court because she had killed Sam, she started to feel as if the scales had fallen from her eyes. That strange trip was a trip out into the country so he could kill her and hide her body. She was completely certain of it. It explained all his behaviour. Telling him she loved him and couldn't stop had saved her life. He simply couldn't do it. Then he toyed with killing both of them in a car crash. But she reminded him of the children and what would happen to them as orphans. She had been in such a state that all of it simply did not register at the time.

They jail van was in the city centre now and soon reached the court. She was weak in the legs with the realisation that Sam had wanted to kill her too, and for the same reason. So that their horrible situation could end. She stumbled as she got down out of the van and a policeman steadied her.

'I'm sorry,' she told him. She really was sorry. For lots of things. 'It's hideous' she mumbled as they walked her into the courthouse. 'Just hideous.'

It seemed they had destroyed each other as surely as if he had committed a murder/suicide on the highway that day.

Once inside the courtroom, she joined Rabinowitz at the table where he was fussing with his notes and files.

'How are you? Bearing up?' he asked her with a kindly smile.

'Yes. I'm okay,' she lied, smoothing her hair.

She still had the gestures of a beauty, though she now felt so battered by life that she was sure only Ben could lust after her. Suddenly, the memory came to her of her and Maya Devereux making their entrance into a club and gliding up to the bar turning every head as they went. There wasn't a man in the place who didn't want them both, singly or together. Maya would say with the arrogance of youth, a glint of pure mischief in her green eyes, 'Look at them. They think it's Christmas.' Maya had died in her youth and beauty when a drunk driver went through a stop sign and collided head-on with her little car. She was only twenty-two, engaged to be married.

Somehow after all that had gone on, it was once again time for the two lawyers to make their closing statements. Clare and Cecilia were in the court dressed to the nines (there was no indication from them that they even knew her), Glenys Davison was there looking ghostly pale, Antonella looked lovely in a peach-coloured suit (she waved and smiled her pretty smile, making Leonora's heart lurch), her father now refused to attend what he described as a 'circus'. Sam's friend Kevin was there glaring at Leonora, as usual. It was like being in a play. It hardly seemed possible that she was the accused, but she was. Maya would have said, 'Are you joking?' with that mad witch's laugh she had.

Pro and Contra

Moira Reynolds got to her feet in a hushed courtroom to make her closing arguments. Not a sound from those assembled in the court. Only the tip-tipping of the court reporter typing a record of the trial and the smooth whoosing of the air conditioning broke the silence.

'Ladies and gentlemen of the jury, there have been stories in the media from time to time that have suggested that Leonora Davison is a monster,' she began. 'I am not here to claim that and I am not here to convince you of that. No. I only claim that she has committed two murders and that she must be held to account as the law demands. My learned friend will tell you the accused didn't know what she was doing the morning of 3 November 1992. That she was in some kind of mental fog, some kind of daze, and is therefore not accountable for what she did. She knew exactly what she was doing because she went there with a gun in her hand to do it. She went there because she was driven by hate, revenge and jealousy. Her ex-husband had abandoned her for another woman and had married that woman and they planned to have a family. The accused found this intolerable. And not only had this other woman taken her husband, because of her the accused had lost a home she treasured, the home where her children had been babies and small children and which she had decorated and turned into a showplace of her fashion sense and good taste and she had also, over time, been separated from her children. Worst of all for someone like the accused, she believed she had been cheated in the financial settlement that resulted from the divorce. Or so she told anyone who would listen. Women have killed for far less,' Reynolds said with a faint smile playing around her lips.

Several jurors didn't like her for that smile.

Blissfully unware of that, she went on. 'Having fallen in love with another woman, Dr Davison ended his marriage. It was, it seems, never a very good marriage but the claims that the doctor beat the accused are not backed up by a shred of evidence. Leonora Davison never went to the police and reported the alleged beatings, there are no police reports and no police photos that back up the claims. Her children never saw her with so much as a bruise. That being the case, you cannot rely on them as mitigation in this case...'

Reynolds talked for three hours. The crux of the matter, she told the jury, was that two murders had been committed and the only way justice could be done for the dead was to find the accused guilty and send her to jail for a long time.

'Were the murders premeditated?' she asked. 'Who could possibly believe they were not when the accused went to the house with a gun, got into the house and shot them both in their bed? She had been to the house previously when Sam and Susan weren't there and she knew where the master bedroom was. Planning and preparation are the clearest indication of premeditation, members of the jury, and there was planning and preparation,' she asserted. 'A woman who does that is not in a mental fog. She is organised and decisive. Like a soldier on a mission into enemy territory, she does reconnaissance. She had already armed herself. Why would she steal the gun? Why would she go and make sure she knew where the master bedroom was in advance? There can be only one reason. She was planning to kill them and that is what she did.'

After urging the jury to find Leonora guilty of premeditated murder, Reynolds closed with the words, 'Those who are merciful to the cruel will end by being cruel to the merciful.' A quote from the Old Testament.

Justice White called a short recess.

Tom Perry had writer's cramp and badly needed coffee. His arse was numb from sitting. He fled the courtroom as if it was on fire and went to the nearest coffee shop to organise his notes. He couldn't see how

Rabinowitz could possibly counter the image Reynolds had created of a cold-blooded killer who planned the crime in advance and carried it out with ruthless efficiency.

Then Rabinowitz got to his feet to fight for Leonora. He had a deep sense of mission with this case such as he had rarely experienced before.

'Members of the jury, this case, on the face of it, seems simple but there are so many strands. So many conflicting versions of events. So many people who say the accused is a bad person, some who claim her husband was and that his new wife was too. But I say to you, members of the jury, it's not that complicated at all. My client has been charged with first-degree murder, which brings with it the necessity of premeditation and that is why I want to acquaint you with some legal concepts.' He swung around to smile at the jury. 'Don't be afraid, gentle jurors,' he said, raising a laugh from the courtroom. 'It's all really quite simple. There is this term in the law, well known to every lawyer but perhaps not so well known to you. *Mens rea*, meaning "guilty mind"; and what exactly does this mean? Basically, it refers to intent. So that you are really clear on the meaning of intent in the legal sense, I want to read something to you. Very briefly.'

Rabinowitz picked up a document from the table in front of him and read, 'In English law, Statute 8, Criminal Justice Act 1967, provides a statutory framework within which *mens rea* is assessed. Now listen closely, members of the jury, because this is very important.' He then read aloud, 'A court or jury in determining whether a person has committed an offence (a) Shall not be bound in law to infer that he (the accused) intended or foresaw a result of his actions by reasons only of its being a natural and probable consequence of those actions, but (b) Shall decide whether he did intend or foresee that result by reference to all the evidence...'

The jurors were hanging on his every word.

'Even more important is the point I wish to make now: the accused may be seen to have a completely different motive to the one ascribed to him or her by the prosecution and if that is the case, then the motive may become subjective evidence that the accused did not intend…' Rabinowitz paused and then repeated, 'Did not intend, but was reckless or wilfully blind.' He paused again to let this percolate in the jurors' minds.

'If my client went to that house on that November morning with a completely different motive for doing so – a motive that did not include the intent to murder, but was reckless and wilfully blind to what the consequence or outcome would be, then there is no intent and if there is no intent such as has been ascribed to my client by the prosecution, then you must find the accused not guilty of first-degree murder. That is the task before you, members of the jury. You must decide: do you believe my client went to that house with the intent to murder or do you believe she went there in such a state of emotional and mental dysfunction that she was reckless and wilfully blind to the possible consequences of going to that house with a gun? Yes, my client chose to go there and to go there armed, but why? That is the question you must answer. And, of course, we have an answer from the accused: she went there with a gun because she had previously been down to the beach with the intention of committing suicide. Her intention was to use the gun to kill herself. Such was her state of mind. She wanted to die. But like so many others before her when it came to the act, she could not carry it out. She then decided to confront her husband and beg him to behave in a just and decent way towards her. She believed with the gun in her hand he would listen to her. This belief was based on desperation, not reason.'

The jury was entranced. Justice White was giving him his full attention too, as were the spectators in the court. Like every brilliant lawyer, he was spinning a web and waiting for the jurors to enter it.

'Another indication of the state of mind of my client is that having left the house on that morning, she was not even aware that she had fired the gun. For almost forty-eight hours after the shooting, she claims she had no memory of shooting the victims. This is what is known as "hysterical amnesia". This is a disorder which typically occurs as an inability to recall traumatic or fear-inducing events: experiences which are linked in the sufferer's mind with guilt, or failure, or rejection. Hysterical amnesia is uncommon, ladies and gentlemen of the jury, but it happens. And here we must turn to the subject of rejection. Rejection is painful, as we all know, but when a woman has been rejected over and over again, over years, by a man she still loves, it can cause an abnormal state of mind and an abnormal emotional reaction. This is what happened to my client. The words "Call the police" were a trigger for her and what they triggered were intense feelings of both rage and rejection. And these are the words my client eventually remembered Dr Davison yelling when he saw her in the bedroom with a gun. Hearing them, it seems she entered what is known as a fugue state, a disassociative state culminating in her hysterical amnesia and the inability to remember for almost forty-eight hours, what had occurred in that bedroom. In this fugue state, a person is disconnected from reality and from their normal identity: and it was in this state that the accused stole her ex-husband's credit card and went on a shopping spree and also picked up a man in a café and went with him to a hotel room. This is a woman who was a virgin on her wedding night. A woman who was completely faithful to her husband while he slept with woman after woman in secret. A woman who had never committed a crime in her life. This kind of behaviour was completely abnormal for Leonora Davison and occurred while she was in this fugue state.'

Even Moira Reynolds was lost in admiration. She considered Rabinowitz with a new-found respect. Or to put it in the terms she used afterwards to her husband, 'I didn't know the little fucker had it in him.'

'To sum up,' said Rabinowitz, fixing the jurors with his gaze. 'If there was no intent on the part of my client to commit murder when she went to that house, then there is no premeditation and she cannot be guilty of first-degree murder. The fact that she had intended to commit suicide shows that she was not fully in control of herself that morning. That she was in a state of heightened anxiety and depression which spiralled out of control when she found a legal document in her letter box telling her that her husband was taking their children to France for possibly six months, which he could do because he had full custody of them. The hysterical amnesia and the out of character behaviour that followed the shootings show she was in a fugue state, a dissociative state and that she was not mentally competent on that day. This also means that she was not able to form clear intent to murder and therefore unable to be guilty of murder. I ask you, members of the jury, to find my client not guilty of this charge. Thank you for your attention.'

He sat down with a flourish of his robes and turned to smile at Lara. She mouthed, 'Well done.'

Justice White then instructed the jury and they left the courtroom and went to their deliberations. The court rose and Justice White made his exit like an actor leaving the stage. The image was reinforced by his matinee idol looks.

Leonora was escorted by guards and taken to a holding cell in the basement of the court. Clare and Cecilia Davison looked enraged. Tom Perry looked dazed. Sam's friend Kevin stared at Rabinowitz with anger and contempt. Then all the spectators filed out into the foyer.

In the empty courtroom, Rabinowitz gathered his papers and files together. Moira Reynolds did the same. They shared a polite smile and left the court.

The Verdict

The jury was out for only two days this time. During that time, Reynolds was philosophical and Rabinowitz was a nervous wreck.

Lara had to stage an intervention when his consumption of black coffee threatened to bring on heart palpitations. 'No more,' she told him. 'You're going to make yourself crazy.'

But then word came that the jury had a verdict and they all made their way to the courthouse.

'Thank God!' Rabinowitz said, throwing on his robe and wig. 'One way or another, it will soon be over. This case has been torture.'

Reynolds looked cool as a cucumber, ready for any eventuality. She sipped a final sip of tea, popped a breath mint and put on her wig and robe.

The judge's associate said, 'Will the foreman please stand.'

He did so, holding a piece of paper in his hand.

'Have you reached a verdict on which the majority of you are agreed?' said the judge's associate.

'We have.'

'On the charge of murder, how do you find the defendant: guilty or not guilty?'

Rabinowitz thought his coffee-drenched heart would leap out of his chest and run out of the courtroom.

'Not guilty,' said the foreman in a flat, emotionless voice and Leonora burst out into loud sobbing.

Her head in her hands, she wept as if her heart would break but Rabinowitz knew that couldn't happen because it had already been broken years before. To his shame, he realised he had tears in his eyes, too.

Justice White told Leonora, 'You're free to go,' adding, 'Court is adjourned,' and he brought his gavel down with finality.

The judge's associate said, 'All rise.'

They did and Justice White left the courtroom and then the court-house on his way to birthday breakfast with his family.

Leonora turned to look at her daughters but they were already walk-ing away and had their backs to her. Antonella came up to her and they embraced. Ben Nolan appeared and also embraced her.

'My daughters…' she sobbed to Nolan.

'Don't worry, they'll come around,' he said. 'You're still their mother.'

Rabinowitz told Leonora that the media were massed at the front door of the courthouse and were in a frenzy. 'It will be better to go out the back way. My junior is waiting with a car.'

Leonora threw her arms around Rabinowitz. 'Thank you. Thank you. I don't know what to say,' she said tearfully, and then she and Nolan and her mother were hustled away to the back door of the court-house to the waiting car.

Lara and Rabinowitz went out the front, partly as a distraction while Leonora made her escape, and he gave a statement to the media but later he couldn't remember a word of what he said.

In the car, Leonora turned to Ben Nolan and said, 'You're stubborn, aren't you?'

'It's the Nolan stubbornness. It's the Irish in me,' he told her.

Antonella gave a baffled laugh. She had no idea what they were talk-ing about. She had never seen Nolan until that moment and didn't have a clue why he was in the car.

The Jurors Speak

Tom Perry had gathered eight of the jurors from Leonora's trial in his dining room. The other four refused to talk to him. He thought it was only fair that they should give their reasons for the verdict they had come to, so it could be included in his book. There they sat at his dining room table, some with mugs of coffee, others with glasses of wine. Three kitchen chairs had been pressed into service because he only had six chairs around his more formal dining room table. He had decided to use a very small tape recorder instead of a notebook. Less distracting. He wanted them to be relaxed, so he had played mine host and done a reasonable job. He was after all a bit of an introvert, as many writers are, so it was a strain. But now, the niceties over and with coffee, biscuits and wine inside them, they were ready to talk.

Jack, a plumber in his forties, was the first to find the courage to say what he knew and what he felt about the case and about the trial. 'She always looked like a real lady to me. I just couldn't believe that she planned it. She seemed to be in a really bad way from what the defence said. For myself, I can only say I wanted to acquit, not right away, but as time went on and as more and more evidence piled up about what kind of man he was and how he had treated her, I didn't feel or believe that she was guilty of first-degree murder and I was glad when the defence lawyer explained about intent and about the amnesia and the fugue state. I've looked it up since on Google, and it only confirmed my belief that she had not planned anything but was kind of caught up in a situation she couldn't control.'

'So you voted to acquit right from the start of deliberations?' Perry asked him.

'Yes, I did.'

'Frances, what about you?'

She was a slender young woman in her twenties with very straight blonde hair and horn-rimmed glasses. Quite conservatively dressed for her age.

'I'm doing a law degree at the moment,' she said. 'Before the closing arguments, I could have gone either way, but after the defence spoke, I was convinced we had to vote to acquit. If we had had the option of manslaughter as a charge, it would have been different, but we didn't. That option wasn't available to us. And the judge had ruled out self-defence as an option too.'

Then a middle-aged woman called Denise had her say. Perry knew she was a receptionist at a doctor's surgery. She had softly waved brown hair, gentle brown eyes and a curvy figure shown to advantage by a clingy brown dress. She looked a bit like a portrait by an artist with a limited palette.

'At first, I was convinced she was guilty but as both sides had their say and called witnesses, I began to doubt that she had committed pre-meditated murder,' she said. 'I think I was a bit like Jack. I wanted to acquit in the end, and the defence lawyer's closing statement convinced me it was the right thing to do.'

'Were you shocked that Dr Davison had been unfaithful, and unfaithful on what can only be described as an epic scale?' Perry asked,

'I suppose it was a surprise. I wouldn't say I was shocked but I had the impression at first that he was a very, well, conservative man and it seems he was nothing of the kind,' Denise said, laughing.

'Did it influence your decision to vote to acquit?'

'I think it did a little bit but mainly I was swayed by the defence lawyer's explanation about intent and the amnesia and fugue state. I didn't believe someone in that state could plan a murder,' she said. 'Or have the intention to murder.'

'I don't think it influenced me,' said Megan – a mother and home-maker, as Perry mused, they called them these days.

'How many children do you have?' Perry asked, hoping it wasn't one of those inappropriate questions that men weren't supposed to ask women.

'I have three boys, four, six and eight,' she rattled off. 'And I can assure you I would be horrified if any of them grew up to be like Sam Davison,' she said, leaning back in her chair as if daring Perry to challenge her on that.

'Could you explain a bit more what you mean by that?' Perry said.

'I think Dr Davison was a disgrace to his gender and his profession. I just don't understand how he could treat his wife, the mother of his children, the way he did. It appalled me when all of that came out in court. And him a doctor!'

'Appalled you? So you disliked Dr Davison?'

'I despised him. He disgusted me,' she said, lifting her chin and looking him in the eye.

'And did you like Leonora Davison?'

'Not particularly. But I believe she was a good wife and mother and she was faithful to her husband and was betrayed by him over and over again. I'm not justifying what she did but, honestly, when all that stuff about the beatings came in, I felt like vomiting. What gave him the right? She was not his property, his slave or some kind of animal, a lesser being that he could treat her like that.'

'Would you describe yourself as a feminist?' Perry asked her, aware he was dealing with delicate issues.

'Not particularly,' she said again. 'I just believe human beings are equal and that kind of treatment of a defenceless woman is outrageous.'

Perry thought to himself, So you are a feminist, you just don't know it.

At that point, Perry replenished the coffee pot, refilled the wine glasses and offered the plate of biscuits around. The talk soon flowed again and with a little less inhibition than before.

The oldest juror was James, a retired pharmacist. He was a clever-looking man with bright blue eyes and a calm demeanour. 'I kept an open mind throughout,' he said. 'I tried to be fair and objective. It was hard when his mistreatment of his wife and his infidelities came in to evidence but I tried simply to focus on the evidence from the day of the shootings. Doing that, and after listening to the prosecution's closing statement, I was not inclined to acquit but like the others I was persuaded by the defence lawyer's closing statement. It put a whole new light on the entire situation at the house the day the shots were fired,' he said, reaching up to stroke his white beard, which matched his white head hair. 'I could not in all fairness say she had intent when she went to the house. I don't believe she did.'

'You were quite sure of that?'

'Yes, I was.'

'So was I,' said Jacinta, a hairdresser in her thirties.

She was pretty but wearing a little bit too much make-up. However, Perry thought to himself, that was probably a professional requirement in her job. Her long hair was lovely: chestnut-brown with a lot of shine and some amber highlights. Perks of the job, no doubt. Her green eyes were softly ringed with kohl and she wore a lot of shiny rings on her fingers, but no wedding band.

'I didn't see how anyone in the state the defence lawyer described could have gone there intending to kill them. She was out of her tree that day, in my opinion. I felt as if I had to vote to acquit.'

'Out of her tree?'

'Absolutely.'

'Not capable of having intent to murder?'

'I don't think so.'

Perry thought more and more that Rabinowitz was probably going to end up a QC.

'And what about you, Tim?'

'Much the same. I really disliked Leonora Davison at first. And in my opinion, she didn't do herself a favour with a lot of her comments in court, so I was not going to acquit but having listened to both the lawyers, I found the defence lawyer's argument more convincing.'

Tim was a musician. He had shoulder-length black hair and blue eyes fringed with thick black lashes. He was skinny, sexy and wearing tight jeans and a sky blue shirt. He had a gold earring in one ear.

'You weren't persuaded by the prosection's closing statement?'

'No. The explanations about intent and the amnesia and the fugue state were very compelling for me. It explained so much about what had happened that day and the things she had done when she left the house, which I couldn't understand at all at first.'

'I agree with Tim. I was never convinced that she acted out of jealousy, either, or hate or any of that. I think she was a desperate woman and not well at all that day and she had just found out that he was taking the kids to France for, was it six months? He didn't need to do that. He was doing it because he could and it was wrong and the unfairness of that pushed her over the edge,' said the last juror at Perry's table: Craig, a self-employed woodworker.

'So she was provoked?'

There was a rumble of agreement around the table.

'Provoked and provoked and provoked,' said Craig.

'But we couldn't consider that, really. We had to just go on what the law told us,' said Jacinta while the others nodded. 'And when the defence lawyer told us what the law said about intent, well, we knew we had to acquit her of the charge, which depended so much on intent or premeditation. I don't think any of us believed she had intent, not when it came to it. And that was it, really.'

'If intent don't fit, you must acquit,' said Tim, cheekily invoking the trial of O.J. Simpson, while the others laughed, not quite sure if they should.

'But don't think we didn't take it seriously. We all did and because we took it so seriously we couldn't convict her of that offence,' said James.

The others nodded.

'The cruelty of that man,' said Megan. 'That he could treat the mother of his children like that, it's just incredible to me.'

'And she was faithful,' said Denise, shaking her head. 'She never cheated on him.'

'But that wasn't a determining factor for me,' Jacinta said, briskly. 'He treated her very badly but when the defence lawyer read out that criminal act, what was it, Statute Eight, about intent, it just all became so clear to me. I had reasonable doubt that she had intent, so I had to vote to acquit.'

Rabinowitz had done a fine job for his client, thought Perry as he heard the last of the jurors' cars drive off and began clearing away glasses and cups and biscuit crumbs.

Then he sat down to listen to the tape and transcribe their comments for his book. He finished off the last of the wine as he wrote. The book was three-quarters done.

Some Light At Last

'See the way she's put that light there on the floor. Spilling in from the open door,' Leonora said. She and Nolan were looking at one of Margaret Olley's paintings in an art book. An interior scene, a room filled with furniture and light.

'I'm still working on being able to do something like that.'

'Well, your paintings sell, so you must be doing something right,' he said.

'Don't they say, never underestimate the bad taste of the public?' she grinned.

'That's a bit hard on your admirers. Is everything hung?'

'Yes, it's all ready for the opening.'

It had been three years since the trial and in that time Leonora had become an artist. She thought now it was what she should have become and would have under different circumstances or if she had been more ambitious for success. Tonight was the opening night of one of her exhibitions. She always invited her children but they never came.

On a side table near the couch was a photo of Kay Tait and her daughter Caitlin: blonde-haired and blue-eyed, like her father, Caitlin was Kay's reason to straighten up and fly right.

'She's my big love,' Kay had told Leonora on the phone, starting to cry.

The photo had been taken at the prison but Kay was out on parole now and Leonora and her kept in touch via email and Skype. Kay still lived in New South Wales but Leonora and Nolan lived in Noosa in Queensland. Kay had been up for one visit and had been amazed that Leonora was now a painter.

'Christ, I never took you for one of them. I never thought you were the artistic type,' she cackled. 'It's pretty, I suppose, your stuff. I like the ones of the sea.'

'Dammed with faint praise,' Leonora said.

'That man of yours is okay, is he? Good to ya?'

'He's mad about me, poor guy. Yes, he's good to me.'

'And good in bed?'

'Kay! You're a shocker,' Leonora said but Kay just screeched with laughter and leered.

She was steering clear of men, she told Leonora. 'I don't trust myself. I'm just goin' to have to have a meanin'ful relationship with George.' George was her Jack Rusell pup. 'Rescued from a rubbish dump, like me,' she said with a rueful chuckle.

The exhibition was at Le Coeur art gallery in Noosa. It was a beautiful space – all white walls and warm golden wood floors. The white walls showed her paintings to great advantage and the lighting in the gallery was superb. She mainly painted landscapes of local scenes. Beach scenes and scenes from up in the mountains at Montville. She loved the feeling of being above everything – even above the clouds – in Montville. Leonora discovered she had a gift for painting clouds, so she was in her element so high up. She had become a 'name' artist in quite a short time, especially considering she hadn't painted since she was at university.

'First infamy and then fame,' she told Kay Tait.

She had no idea if her notoriety as a murderess had contributed to her success. If the buyers saw her as a sinner (how they loved those) redeemed by art, she had no idea. No one said it but who could know what was going on in the minds of those who snapped up her paintings? They cost thousands but that didn't discourage them at all. Their motives were not her concern and as long as she could make a living from painting she didn't care about their motives either.

Ben and she shared a double-storey white stucco house near the beach with a pool and a gym where she worked out daily. She had her figure back and always had a light tan to complement her blue eyes and blonded hair. Ben followed her with his eyes whenever she walked into a room – and when she left. Sometimes she teased him about his 'crush' and even though she would never love him the way she had loved Sam, she sometimes thought that was probably for the best. 'Look how that ended,' she would think, watching Ben's tanned, muscular body as he went about some mundane task. She especially loved watching him stack the dishwasher and when he bent over, she would sometimes sneak up on him and run her hands all over his arse.

'Stop it,' he would, say very seriously. 'You'll make me break something.'

And she would laugh at him and back him up against a wall so she could kiss him. It wasn't love, because she knew how love felt, but it was a peaceful harbour and he was great in bed. She had no complaints.

Time to dress. Showtime, as she thought of it. Her hair was long now and hung in waves around her face: she never straightened it any more. She put on a peach-coloured sheath dress and hung a heavy gold necklace she had designed herself around her neck. Simple gold stud earrings went in her ears and strappy gold sandals on her feet.

'Can we go to bed?' Ben said, slipping his hands inside the dress to play with her breasts.

'You know damn well we can't,' she told him, kissing him to soften her words.'There's no time. I can't be late.'

'After, then, when you return in triumph,' he said holding her against him.

'Yes, that will be lovely,' she said, kissing him again.

They toasted to the success of the exhibition with champagne. One glass each. Then they got into her pink sports car (it was a mindless extravagance, but what the hell, she wasn't going to live forever) and drove to the gallery.

The car park next to the art gallery was packed as they drove in. All the lights were blazing in the gallery and there were people wall to wall moving around with glasses of wine in their hands.

'Looks good,' said Ben.

'Looks very good. Let's get in there.' Leonora got out and started walking.

'Soldier, soldier wait for me,' said Ben, catching up.

'Sorry, sweetie. I just hate being late for an exhibition.'

They swept in through the glass doors and heads turned. Most of the prospective buyers were clutching the glossy brochure that had been put out for the exhibition. It had a photo of Leonora on the front cover and one of her paintings, of the sea near Noosa, featured too. A photographer hovered and Ben put his arm around her and smiled as the flash went off. He was becoming an expert at posing for the camera.

Antonella and Carlo came over and hugged them.

'You look beautiful, Leo,' Antonella said.

'So do you. Green is your colour,' Leonora told her.

'I'll take another,' said the photographer and Leonora was glad. She had a habit of blinking when the flash went off.

He was from the local paper. There was going to be an article on the exhibition. The name on the paintings hanging on the walls of the gallery was Leonora Morelli, not Davison. Her personal favourite of these paintings was of the moon shining on the sea and whimsical sea creatures drifting in the dark ocean. She had predicted it would sell early and when she went over to look at it, there was a red dot on it.

'Sold! I told you,' she said to Ben.

'You know I'm not much on art,' he laughed. 'But I can see the sign with the price. Kaaaching.

'Barbarian,' Leonora said.

'But I'm your barbarian, aren't I?' he grinned and pulled her to him.

The next morning, after they had waved goodbye to Antonella and Carlo, Ben suggested they go into Noosa and have breakfast.

'Yes, let's do that,' Leonora said.

It was a coffee shop and a bookshop combined. While waiting for the coffee, Leonora wandered around the bookshelves and then stopped dead.

There it was. Tom Perry's book, *The Golden Couple*, stared at her from one of the shelves. She had avoided the book. Had never read it. Sam and her were on the front cover in their wedding outfits with a white zigzag splitting them apart. That beautiful girl and that handsome man had harmed each other in ways they could never have imagined. She felt weak and nauseous. Her face was covered in beads of sweat and she thought she was going to faint. She wiped her hand across her forehead.

Ben appeared next to her. 'Do you want to buy it?' he said in all innocence, unaware of the state she was in.

'No, I don't,' she said angrily.

'It's about you. Don't you want to read it?'

'Is it?' she said, finding it hard to breathe. 'It's not, you know. It's about someone who used to be me. She died when he did and she's not coming back,' she told him, faintly, holding on to the bookshelves to stay on her feet. Tears ran down her face but she never made a sound.

'Are you okay, darl? You look awful.' Ben took hold of her and steered her back to the table where their coffees sat waiting. 'Drink some coffee,' he said.

She put her head down on the table.

'Sweetie? Are you okay?' he ran his hand up and down her back in a soothing gesture.

She realised she had never cried for Sam. Now, after burying it for so long, there it was. The grief, the shame and the pain.

A waitress came over and said, 'Is she okay?'

'She'll be fine, we just need a moment,' Ben told her.

The waitress retreated.

Eventually, Leonora started sipping her coffee between sobs.

'Have some carrot cake, you need the sugar,' Ben said putting a forkful into her mouth.

She swallowed it with difficulty. 'I'm sorry. I don't want to make a fuss,' she said. But the thought of being the centre of a fuss made her think of Maya Devereux and she started crying again. Her whole life was beginning to flash before her eyes – but only the bad parts.

'Do you want to go?'

'No. If I start running away, I'll never stop.' She sipped the coffee and gradually calmed down. 'Seeing that damn book threw me, but I remember now,' she said with determination. 'I'm Leonora Morelli, Leonora Davison is gone.' She wiped her tears away with her hands and blew her nose on a serviette.

Everyone was glancing at them and some were staring but she was not going to leave.

'Give me that cake,' she said and Ben pushed the plate over to her. She ate it all, still sobbing.

They went home and made love, slowly, while the ocean rushed rhythmically outside the window. He kissed her as he moved on top of her until she came and then he kissed her again. They spent the rest of the day in bed.

At sunset, she set up her easel and paints and started painting the one thing she had never captured to her satisfaction on canvas: the colours of the sky as the sun sets. Ben slept on as she painted. She piled the paint on her palette and set to work. Nature, that brilliant artist, did the same.

In spite of her determination not to remember anything about it, she remembered going into the house, she remembered the feel of the gun in her hand, she remembered their screams and the blood and Sam cowering in fear, his pallor, the sweat on his upper lip. She had never seen him like that before. It shocked her but she couldn't help herself, couldn't stop. She fired the gun again and again. That would always be there. In her head. She would live with it forever. A life sentence.

Brilliant oranges flowed from her brush and some golds and creams. She painted huge clouds tinged with gold and orange and slashed some blood red below them. She had to stop for a while and take some deep breaths. Red affected her that way. The painting took shape. She was happy with the progress she had made. She wiped her hands and put the used brushes in turpentine.

Then she went back to Ben and took her clothes off. She rolled against his naked body and breathed in his warmth, and waited for the cold, dead feeling to go. He woke, put his arms around her, gathered her in and kissed her. She came back from the land of the dead and put her hand on his penis, snuggled into his neck.

After they made love again. Ben said, 'Sweetie, let's go out for dinner. You sold all those paintings. The exhibition is a big success. We need to celebrate. You can dress up,' he said.

'That would be nice. Let's go to Sails.'

At Sails, they toasted in champagne.

'What will we toast?' Ben said.

'To art,' Leonora said.

'To art. What else?' Ben said, laughing.

She was having dinner with him and with Sam. Sam was always there. A ghost at every feast. Sometimes she even saw him. Or heard his laugh in the street. But it was never him. He was gone and he wasn't coming back. Was he in some other world with her? Even dead, Susan Ross haunted her. She was still jealous. Even in the afterlife – if there was one – Susan Ross had no right to her husband. And he would always be her husband, forever and forever. As she told him on their wedding night. And that was a vow she kept.

About the Author

Antonia Hildebrand is a poet, short story writer and essayist. She was born and educated in Toowoomba, Queensland. She married Reinhard Hildebrand in the early seventies and moved with him to Hamburg, Germany. She lived and worked in Europe for three years and also travelled in Europe and Asia before returning to Australia. She then studied at the Toowoomba Technical College, going to evening classes before gaining admission to the University of Queensland and graduating Bachelor of Arts in 1987 with a major in English literature. In 1993 she graduated Master of Letters (German) from the University of New England. Her first published short story, 'Nothing Ever Happens', appeared in *Woman's Day* in 1981 and *Downs Images* in 1982 and she has since been widely published in journals, magazines and anthologies in Australia as well as Britain and the USA. Her poems have appeared in *Coppertales, Iodine Poetry Journal, Poetrix, Harvester* and *Squidink*. From 2000 to 2002 she was a member of Crime Writers Queensland and had two stories published in their books – 'The Weeping Madonna' in *Menace in the Mulga* and 'Second Nature' in *Bad to the Bones*. Her short stories have appeared in *Downs Images, Woman's Day, Shortz, First Edition Magazine, Tirra Lirra* and *Four W Seventeen*. An essay on John Howard, 'Ordinary Australians', was published in *Overland* in 2003.

In 1998 she won the University of Southern Queensland Library Poetry Prize and in 1999 the Fellowship of Australian Writers' Marjorie Barnard Short Story Award. In 2002 she began contributing to Radio National's *Bush Telegraph* program. Many of her short stories have been broadcast by *Queensland Storyteller* on Radio 4RPH and by *Words and Music* on Radio 91.3 FM. Her Radio National pieces and her film reviews and essays were collected for her book *The Past is Another Country: Viewpoints, Essays & Reviews* published in 2003. She has also explored growing to adulthood, living in Europe and returning to Australia in the years 1951 to 1975 in her memoir *Beautiful Life*. In 2004 she co-wrote, with John Boshammer, *Boshy and Me*, a biography of his rugby legend father, Kev Boshammer. A poetry collection, *The Sweet Time*, was published in 2006. Other publications include *The Blind Colossus*, an essay collection, 2015; *To Breathe and Other Stories*, 2016; *War Stories*, a poetry collection, 2017; and *A Simple Twist of Fate*, 2020. She was elected president of the Fellowship of Australian Writers Queensland (2015–2016).